GENERATIONS

Mission Statement

This is an initiative of the Tamil Nadu Textbook and Educational Services Corporation (TNTB & ESC) under the aegis of one of the announcements for the year 2021-22, titled "Thisaidhorum Dravidam" by Honourable Minister for School Education Thiru. Anbil Mahesh Poyyamozhi to identify and translate into English, Kannada, Malayalam and Telugu, Tamil literary works, that they might enhance the reach of Tamil antiquity, tradition and contemporaneity and enrich World literature and to also translate significant literary voices from other Dravidian languages into Tamil. Both ventures are to be undertaken as either independent or joint publications with collaborating publishers.

GENERATIONS

Talaimuraikal

NEELA PADMANABHAN

WINNER OF SAHITYA AKADEMI AWARD
& SARASWATI SAMMAN

Translated from the Tamil Original by
Ka. Naa. Subramaniam

THORNBIRD
NIYOGI BOOKS

Published by
NIYOGI BOOKS
Block D, Building No. 77,
Okhla Industrial Area, Phase-I,
New Delhi-110 020, INDIA
Tel: 91-11-26816301, 26818960
Email: niyogibooks@gmail.com
Website: www.niyogibooksindia.com

Editor: Mini Krishnan
Design: Shashi Bhushan Prasad
Cover design: Misha Oberoi

ISBN: 978-93-91125-04-2
Publication: 2021
Reprint: 2024

Printed at: Niyogi Offset Pvt. Ltd., New Delhi, India

Introduction

It is from these elements—story, people, and rhythm identified by E.M. Forster, that a good novel is put together. When the spirit of the "navarasas" (the classical Indian nine-fold quintessence of emotion) combine felicitously, you have an authentic Indian novel. *Talaimuraikal* (*Generations*) begins and ends on a note of peace and auspiciousness, and in between is a taste of the fullness of human experience. Not many modern Indian novels have achieved this balance.

Generations is a story of generational change and conflict and of how a boy grows up to take charge of a family which has loved its traditions not wisely, but too well. Neela Padmanabhan wrote it at the end of the 1960s, setting it some 25 years earlier. The many - branched plot, with big and little stories flowering on every twig, is rooted in the life of a single community—the Tamil speaking Chettis of Eraniyal town in the southernmost part of India, Kanyakumari District, on the border of modern Kerala. In the 1940s, this was still a part of the princely state of Malayalam-speaking Travancore (now southern Kerala). The Tamil that is spoken here has a Malayalam lilt and many Malayalam phrases and idioms, but the Chettis of the "Seven Towns", as they call themselves, think of themselves as Tamils, with a distinctive culture. The wider Malayali society does, however, impinge on the claustrophobic milieu of the migrant Chettis. It offers an escape valve for the rich and bored (as in the case of the young Koonangani, who takes a Nair mistress), or a haven to those who, like Kuttalam, are the victims of ostracism.

The novel is an original and fresh distilling of the indigenous tradition of orature, a distinct art form in this region with practitioners, such as the Brahmin Bhagavathars, the Oduvars or temple-reciters, and the Therukoothu (street theatre) players relating stories from the epics and the Puranas. Storytelling thrived within the family, with older members using ancestral history and legend to reinforce favoured attitudes and values.

This genre used, not the formal written Tamil, which is standardised, but oral Tamil, which varies from district to district and between castes and communities. In the book's many fine passages, Neela Padmanabhan raises this common speech of Eraniyal Chettis to the level of poetry, incorporating proverbs and idioms, humorous and witty anecdotes, and several kinds of folk songs, from droll nonsense rhymes to sonorous dirges. Because the writer has chosen the spoken form, his Tamil has escaped the tendency to pedantry and affectation observable in some forms of literary Tamil. Here the borrowings of the dialect from Malayalam and English are "tamilised" with an instinctive ear for the euphony peculiar to Tamil.

Though *Generations* is an intricate tale, it is simply told. The reader has a restful feeling of being in the hands of a master, because its particularities are meticulously delineated against the background of language, myth, and ethnic consciousness. In the original, the effect is like being led into a cave where time and space have been compressed. Your pupils slowly expand to take in the surrounding frescoes, executed with pigments that you recognise immediately as taken from the earth that is common to all, although you may be from another part of it. Character after character comes alive for you, as you share the vision of the author-protagonist.

The theme is the dilemma of the individual who is faced with two needs—one, to cleave to a nurturing tradition, and another, to redress an injustice that receives sanction in that tradition. A third need—to make one's way independent of the tradition—remains suppressed till the end, when changed circumstances dislodge it and set it free, as the wind might loosen a seed stuck in a dry spot.

The novel describes the immiseration of a family and a caste, leading to migration. Family legends preserve the experience of uprooting and migrations within the southern country. These "little migrations over relatively smaller distances than those across the seas" disprove the stereotype of "unchanging India". Many families, even in the relatively more stable South, have a history of having come from "somewhere else", carrying with them an irreducible minimum of cultural baggage, which will affirm their distinct identity.

Young Diravi, descendant of a clan of small trader-farmers of the Chetti caste who had migrated from Tamil

Nadu to the princely state of Travancore centuries earlier, has imbibed throughout his childhood certain socialising values along with his grandmother's stories of a vanished glory.

When his parents decide to get their daughter, Nagammai, married into a wealthy family (so that she will always have "a fully belly"), Diravi comes face to face with another and less attractive face of tradition. It is the face of Papati, the grasping mother-in-law. It is the face of Sevantha Perumal, the son-in-law, who gets away with dismissing one wife to marry another. It is also the face of Unnamalai Aachi, the honoured grandmother, who deeply believes it is wrong for Nagu to be set free from her non-functional marriage to marry another man.

Is the double standard an inescapable result of the adherence to the age-old virtue of honour and chastity (*karpu*) on which the Chettis, like all true Tamils, are supposed to pride themselves? The question can only be articulated properly by one who has looked closely at the stuff of their lives—their livelihood, their beliefs and habits, customs and rites.

Suffering the insult of his sister's rejection, along with his parents and grandmother, Diravi becomes extraordinarily sensitive and observant.

The novel is peopled by dozens of characters, young and old, each of whom appears to Diravi to be a curiously dynamic natural creation. He discovers that it is not so much material circumstances, but a person's cast of mind that seems to really determine his or her behaviour. It is a wonder to him how his grandmother, Unnamalai Aachi's lifelong widowhood and poverty have not soured her or depleted her energy. She is described in loving detail from her *vibhuti* (holy ash)-smeared forehead and her huge earlobes, with their dangling *paambadam*s (large gold ear-ornaments in a cluster of geometric shapes, which are worn with pride by elderly women of the southern districts of Tamil Nadu) down to her "elephant leg" afflicted with filariasis. Not only does this redoubtable woman have a large and imposing nose that says "Here I am! Look at me!", but she also has a palpable sense of the "soul" of her community. She works hard all day long, assists and advises everyone around her, tells stories to her grandchildren, and sleeps soundly, having delegated all her sorrows to God. Her cherished beliefs and her misgivings about new ways form a vantage point from which Diravi appraises life, and from which he must descend and eventually depart.

It is Unnamalai Aachi who tells of the glory of Chetti women who have been sacrificed for the sake of *karpu*, like the legendary Chetti sisters, whose cleverness cost them dearly. Their descendants are Diravi's sisters—one, a fulfilled wife and mother, another, a *vaazhavetti* (lifeless, discarded wife); and a third girl-child, whose carefree childhood ends at puberty when she must recede into the *saappu* (the darkest corner of the house).

There are also regressive women like Papathi, Nagu's rich mother-in-law, who has driven out her sick husband, and Thayi, the wife who leaves her husband, because he has lost all his money. A poor man like Diravi's father agonises over having to make lavish gifts to his daughter's mother-in-law at every stage of her wedding, but puts up with it all for the sake of caste and family honour. But another poor man, Kuttalam, is driven to defy the community. He befriends men of other castes, thus threatening the caste cohesion so prized by these migrants. Some men grow in statute with suffering, like old Koonangani Paatta, when his wife and sons desert him; others lose their dignity, like the bankrupt and disgraced Kolappan.

The Centrality of Ceremony

Chettis throw themselves into the observation of rites and ceremony, abandoning all caution and frugal instinct; in fact, all their other anxieties and concerns, as soon as any festive opportunity presents itself. It is believed that to hand back, when an auspicious moment is at hand, is to spurn Lakshmi, the Goddess of Fortune. Nagu is married off as soon as a wealthy bridegroom turns up for her, for a wedding is by definition an auspicious event.

Rites strengthen bonds and establish hierarchies of power; they give vent to creative as well as destructive energies. A ceremony initiates the bride Nagu into household tasks, another announces Salam's attainment of puberty, a third blesses Diravi's oldest sister, before she delivers her first child, a fourth orchestrates the rejoicing at the baby's first morsel of solid food. Sixteen days of ceremonies, punctuated by dirges, exorcise the grief felt by all at Unnamalai Aachi's death. Ceremonies weld the community together in the face of their special goddess,

Nagammai, after whom the luckless Nagu has been named. At the Oduparai festival, held once in 12 years, Diravi finds himself "seized by a strange ecstasy of devotion". The reader can almost taste the special, sacred *kozhukattai* of rice-flour, fruit, coconut, and jaggery ("with not a drop of water added"), baked by the Chetti families in underground pits in the open field, where Goddess Nagammai has stood ever since the Chettis arrived here, fleeing from a king's rage.

Diravi's Awakening

These and other fantastic and lyrical episodes in the collective consciousness of the Chettis are, for Diravi, a kind of continuous dream, from which he periodically jerks awake. At the end of the festival, after honouring the idol of *karpu*, comes the news that a widow has run off with her lover, and Diravi awakens once again to the implications of the double standard of sexual morality. The town council (the caste panchayat), which is supposed to guard the identity and the honour of the group, finds it convenient to please the rich Sevantha Perumal.

Unnamalai Aachi, grieved by Nagu's situation, can get to sleep at night, because she simply "leaves it all to God", but Diravi feels the need for meaningful action. Aware as he is of the complexities and contradictions, he never forgets that he is a cherished offshoot of his community. This gives him the credentials to diagnose and to attempt to heal its great sickness of spirit. His weak parents and his neighbours are "frogs-in-a-well"—they cannot help him. It is outside the community, in the person of Moses, the Malayali Christian, that he finds some practical advice. When he begins to act on it, however, he is soon weighed down by a sense of doom. How calamity actually strikes, and brings not only an almost divine retribution in its wake, but also the possibility of freedom and peace, are masterfully told. The novel ends as it begins, with an obeisance to Singa Vinayaka, the tutelary deity of the Eraniyal Chettis.

Because Neela Padmanabhan does not wriggle away from Diravi's dilemma into the literary mode of subjective expressions, the novel stays on course. He does not squander his narrative resources, and every word, image, and anecdote has a bearing on Diravi's development. A work of great imaginative power, this is also a realistic story of how social change has sometimes taken place in India.

How Diravi prepares himself, consciously as well as unconsciously, to fight for what he judges to be his sister's interests, is a reflection of the actual struggle of gender justice that several progressive men have waged on behalf of women. That Nagu has not a word to say for herself throughout the novel is in itself an implicit statement of women's status. Some men have felt that injustice keenly. Though Diravi has no pretensions to become a crusader or a social reformer, he does become his sister's defender. Brotherly chivalry, a common theme in Indian fiction and cinema, is handled convincingly here, without a trace of sentimentalism.

Vasantha Surya

One

The early dawn was cold with the Singa Vinayaka temple[1] tolled for the first puja of the day and the waves of sound, when they reached the long street stretching from east to west, had lost much of their volume and turbulence, retaining only their somewhat spiritual urgency.

The two rows of houses in the street facing each other were small and old-fashioned. True, there were signs of modernity in ungainly patches of colour, newly and thickly laid on. But modern conveniences like electricity had not touched the street at all.

At one end of the street, facing north, was an old, small house. It had a single wooden door blackened and infested with termites. Beyond the door was a passage bordered on both sides by raised verandahs—the verandah on your left as you entered being the smaller one. The big, broad verandah on the right was smeared with cowdung. Unnamalai Aachi[2] was lying on her side on the right verandah and woke up when the temple bells began to ring, saying as was her custom, "O Lord, Singa Vinayaka, my God," mixing it with succeeding yawns, stretching her limbs, then sitting up and stretching her legs before her.

The first thing Unnamalai Aachi took care to see on waking up were the fronds of the coconut-palm rising against the lightening sky over the inner open quadrangle, though the palm was not yet clearly visible in the weak light of dawn. She believed that it was auspicious to see the palm fronds first thing in the morning. "Isnt the coconut tree the *karpaga*[3]—the all giving tree?"

Her legs were stiff with the cold and one of them was affected by elephantiasis—the gift of her baths in the river, Valli, in her younger days as she told all who would listen to her on the subject. The leg had grown bigger with each monthly succession of lymphatic fever. It was fair, bright and shiny, both because of the oil rubbed onto it and the natural colour of the woman herself. Unceasing work had made her strong and thickset, though, now, with age, she was losing weight. Her legs hurt all the time. On rising in the morning, she massaged her legs from toe to thigh with a skill and ease born of daily habit.

Aachi's adored grandson, Diravi, was trying to ward off the cold by curling up inside his blanket. He was lying on the same verandah as the old woman. "Paatti, is it already 5?" he asked, freeing only his mouth reluctantly from the enveloping blanket. "Yes…darling, get up. Children, get up and start reading your books." The old woman paused in the massaging of her legs to say just this and renewed the exercise with greater vigour.

"Isnt it cold? Freezing cold? Don't you feel it Aachi?" asked the boy, Diraviam, expressing his reluctance to get up.

"Eh! Eh! This body has known the greatest cold of the world. You are young and tender, only just sprouting and you feel the cold more than I do." She adjusted the blanket over her grandson where it had slipped a little. After that she resumed her massage.

She would continue massaging her legs for at least 15 minutes and then get up. Once on her feet, she continued working till she lay down to sleep at 11 or 12 or sometimes, even later. "My Lord Singa Vinayaka!" she would say and go to bed, stretching her limbs languidly.

Her hair was white and scanty. Her forehead, adorned with sacred ash, had a permanent discolouration, like smudges of ash. Her eyes were sunken, her lips dry and thin. Her nose with flaring nostrils rose majestically on her face. Smallpox marks pitted her face and her earrings were never still, except when she slept. This was the distinctive face that was Unnamalai Aachi. Diraviam was reminded of the shrunken pickled mango, whenever he saw Aachi's face. "As long as I can remember, Aachi has been wearing these kinds of white clothes[4]. Why doesn't she wear coloured clothes or, like Mother or sister, a blouse?" he used to ask himself, whenever he saw her bending over, doing some work or the other.

Beyond the passage was the courtyard. Beyond the courtyard in the house was a raised verandah, on which rose two wooden pillars worn thin by household members rubbing their backs on it to relieve their itching. On a mat on the verandah lay Diraviam's father, Nagaru Pillai. He woke up saying loudly, “Lord…Vignesware[5],” and sat up on the mat, stretching his limbs.

He was 45 years old. His hair was still black. Though there was frustration and defeat on his face, there was also something else—a kind of serenity.

“Dorai has neither my face nor features nor body…he is like his father,” was Unnamalai Aachi’s proud boast. Dorai’s was a strong body made stronger by constant labour. Nagaru Pillai, Aachi’s son, was named after his grandfather, Aachi’s father-in-law, whose name she would not use; so, she always referred to her son as Dorai.

“Amma…hasn’t Diravi got up yet? Wake him up and ask him to read.”

Nagaru stood in the courtyard, tying his dhoti properly, his voice hoarse and unclear with sleep.

“He, poor fellow, feels the cold. Let him sleep a little more,” muttered his mother, but her words did not reach him at all.

Nagaru went to the second door, which sealed off the inner rooms, and knocked on it.

This door was a small one, set in the wall of the verandah. It was adjoined by two even smaller doors. To get into the inner rooms, one had to squat and bend low to avoid knocking one’s head against the lintel. There was an explanation for such a small entrance into the inner rooms, which was a common sight in the houses of the street.

When the men and the older women of a house were out, the young ones and the maidens left behind were expected to close the inner door and keep safe inside. If anyone came in search of the men or the older women of the house, the maidens were expected to reply without opening the door. If they had to open the door, only one of the three leaves of the door was to be opened and anyone from the outside could get only a glimpse of the ankles of the girl within. Theoretically, the ankles might be visible, but if the visitor was standing outside in the light and the girl in the dark within, the visitor could not even glimpse the ankles of the girls of the house.

"Hey, Kuttiamma, open the door," Nagaru shouted.

There were jobs to do in the morning. It was evident in his matter and in the urgency in his voice and tone.

There was the sound of latches being removed. The door, at least six inches thick, opened with loud creaks, reluctantly, as it were.

Opening the door, Kuttiamma stood aside. Nagaru went into the room thick with the smell of stagnant air and the warmth generated in closed spaces.

The draft of cold air pouring in attacked the 10-year old Visalam who was sleeping directly behind the door. She tossed on her mat, muttering something indistinctly, and returned to her dreams. "Daughter Salam…this girl, even in her sleep, talks of play with her friends. She muttered something about games…" said the father with fond severity and opened the rear door.

There was a small square just beyond the rear door. The adjacent verandah had a large roof, which covered the kitchen to the right. To the left, like a giant, stood the granary.

Passing by the granary, Nagaru opened yet another door and taking some burnt chaff (to clean his teeth) from a bucket that hung conveniently, stepped down into the backyard and broke off a green coconut frond to scrape his tongue.

The dewdrops clinging to the blades of grass touched his unshod feet and, in concert with the cold wind, made him shiver. The mango trees were in bloom, spreading a heady scent in the air bringing him a taste of new life.

Inside, Kuttiamma covered Visalam with a cloth, so that the cold draft would not affect her and went into the kitchen to remove the ashes of yesterday's fire from the oven. The ashes spread over her head like a halo.

Pots and pans darkened with soot, along with other utensils of various kinds, had to be cleaned. Kuttiamma took them and spread them by the well. She drew some water and dipping coconut coir into the ashes, scrubbed the bottoms and the insides of the vessels. She washed each one meticulously, the bangles on her forearm tinkling against the vessels.

By this time, Unnamalai Aachi would have finished massaging her legs. She would draw the stone and pestle and the betelnut plate towards her and, preparing the betel leaves, nuts, and quicklime, she would begin knocking them into suitable shapes. This had a special rhythm with which everyone in the house was familiar; she would do it once or twice even when half-asleep in the night, and often during the day. It formed a rhythmical pattern of sound in the ears of her dear grandson.

Before she could wake him up again, he rose. The early dawn was dark in patches where he lay. In the dark, he groped for the matchbox and lit the chimney lamp. He searched in his box for his book and, stretching his legs on to the opposite platform, began to read where the book opened, sleepily mumbling the words.

Aachi got down from the verandah, took a small bucket from a corner of the courtyard and went to the well at which Kuttiamma was washing the vessels.

"Kutti...you are up...? Dorai wanted to be reminded that he had to go to Kurunthankode fields this morning...give him some cold rice-water before he starts. The other day he went without eating anything and came back complaining of feeling faint..." So saying, Aachi drew water from the well for her own use.

Her daughter-in-law Kuttiamma said, "Yes, I shall give him something to eat. Is the boy up and reading without a beating from his father?"

"He has been reading for some time now," Aachi replied, and came back to the courtyard with a bucket of water in her hand.

"There is a famine of cowdung...What a famine! This was a house in which we kept a whole herd of cows, buffaloes, and calves. Now we have to beg for cowdung from inferior people. The head-shaking old woman comes every day to collect our kitchen refuse, but she will not bring cowdung in exchange, however often you tell her. The small ones of the world have become great!" The old woman's name was Ekki;

her head trembled with both age and general weakness, so everybody renamed her the "head-shaking old woman". She too had no objection to that appellation.

Aachi was talking to no one in particular. She was merely expressing her own discontent with the state of things in general. There was a little cowdung in the corner of the courtyard; she mixed it with the water in the bucket[6] and came out of the house to the front, opening the outer door. The cold wind attacked the inside of the house like sharp needles.

Two

The eastern sky was getting lighter by the minute. Diravi brought his lamp to the street and, dangling his legs from the verandah, sat, book in hand, with the chimney light beside him.

He was aware that those who saw him thus would make fun of him, saying that he wanted others to see him reading. But his being there served a dual purpose. It was useful for him as well as for granny, who was sweeping the street in front of the house. So, it was his daily habit to sit like that, reading.

As far back as Diravi could remember, Aachi had cleaned and moistened the street in front of their house every morning with great concentration. It was almost as if she undertook it as a task of great artistic skill. And he loved to watch her doing it. First, she would sweep the front with the stiffer and shorter bundle of thin sticks; then, she would make a rhythmic music by sprinkling the street with the cowdung-and-water mixture. No one could sleep through that steady and insistent sound. After moistening the ground with the cow-dung water, she would sweep the street once again with a longer and thinner broom. In the midst of reading the book in hand, Diravi would suffer many doubts and anxieties about what went on in the world.

It was at such times that he would voice his doubts loudly, so that Aachi could resolve them. He would thus get to learn the stories, traditions, customs and habits of the community into which he had been born. A daily opportunity to improve his stock of general and common knowledge.

Diravi was 15 years old. Four or five years ago, he had learnt that if lightning struck a cowdung pit, the cowdug would turn into solid gold. From the same source he had heard that serpents had in their heads what was called the "serpent germ". Dawn was the hour in which such open secrets and ancient lore were passed on by Aachi to her grandson.

Something had been nagging Diravi from the evening before. He now brought it up.

"Aachi...in our caste, no one has so far been bitten by a snake…no, no, I mean a rope and died. Right?"

To mention the word "snake", when it was not yet broad daylight, was something which Aachi did not like or allow. The boy had said "snake", but corrected it immediately to "rope". If one uttered the word "snake" (according to Aachi) in the dark, a snake would inexorably take shape beside one; if one had to refer to a snake, one used euphemisms like "rope" or indicated it by signs.

"We are the Seven Towns' Chettis. Our family deity is Odupparai, Goddess of the Snake. It will not bite us."

"Seven Towns' Chettis, are we?"

"Yes child, seven towns..." the old woman began to enumerate the seven towns, "Eraniyal, Pazhavadai, Pappanapuram, Parakkai, Midalam...how many does that come to?"

Diravi had been counting the names as the old woman said them and replied that they were five.

"Five..." She removed the broom from the ground, tightened the string around the sticks together, rotated the broom to tighten the hold of the string and, like a schoolboy trying to remember his multiplication table by repeating it to himself, she repeated to herself the five names again and said, "Yes Kolachal, Tiruvankode...that makes seven, doesn't it?" she asked her grandson proudly.

"Yes. But do our caste's people live only in these seven towns?" he asked.

"Nowadays, to earn their living, they have gone to many places. But the families which came from Kaveripoompattinam to this Eraniyal East Street, lived in these seven."

Diravi did not understand completely. Kaveripoompattinam—how did it come into the picture of seven towns?

The old woman was splashing cowdung water on the street with practised skill, raising rhythmic sounds; this was the second part of the morning ceremony.

Why mention Kaveripoompattinam? What has it to do with us?"

"Eh? Child, it is a long story. It cannot be told in a day; I shall tell you later in the night."

Aachi's attempt to put him off only served to make him all the more anxious to hear the story, "You tell me a part of it now, and the other part later," he suggested eagerly.

Darkness was fading from both the earth and sky. Meanwhile, Visalam had also woken up, and come to the street front, dutifully carrying her book. She sat next to Diravi, after putting out the light.

"Eh Salam, you too are awake already?" he asked, surprised.

People were beginning to pass along the street. In the neighbouring houses also, women appeared with brooms and buckets of cowdung - water to clean their street fronts. The temple was celebrating a festival and the *nadaswaram*[1], audible from a distance, was sweet to the ear.

Aachi had finished sprinkling the street with cowdung - water and was engaged in the third and final part of her act.

"A long, long time ago, there was, very far to the north, a city called Kaveripoompattinam. A king ruled over this northern and distant city."

The old woman alternated her narration with vigorous sweeps of her broom. Diravi and Salam listened intently.

"One day, this king was the recipient of a gift of precious coral."

"Coral is like a gem, isn't it?" asked Salam.

"Do you think that coral is a gem like the gems you wear round your neck? Coral is very costly, like diamonds or pearls, isn't it Aachi?" Diravi asked, proud to display the little knowledge he had of these things, simultaneously intent on making fun of Salam for her colossal ignorance.

Aachi was intent on recovering two of the sticks that had got dislodged from her broom. After tightening the string of the broom, she swept the ground vigourously. Meanwhile, the "head-shaking old woman", who was sweeping her frontyard, two doors off, asked, "Oh Unnamalai, the day has dawned and you have begun telling your grandchildren stories."

"The children ask eagerly..." and not willing to let an opportunity like that slip away, she added, "there is no cowdung in the house. When you come to collect the refuse, bring some cowdung. Don't forget."

Diravi was impatient. For him the "head-shaking old woman" had no right to interfere. "You tell us the story. Please continue," he pleaded.

"Eh, where did I stop?" Aachi asked.

"The king was given some corals." Salam was in a hurry to establish her readiness and brightness in comparison with her brother.

"Yes, children. Small corals, enough to make a string, were gifted to the king. They were so bright that they dazzled everyone. The king wanted to string them into a necklace for his queen, who was no less anxious to wear them. But the corals were unpierced."

"The king was deceived by a gift of unpierced corals of no worth," Salam pitied the poor king aloud.

"Won't you keep quiet? Don't interrupt as if you are an adult...you continue granny...at last..." Diravi admonished his sister.

"What happened at last? All the goldsmiths of the kingdom examined the corals and tried their skill. But the corals were so small that piercing them looked well-nigh impossible. If they used a needle to pierce them, that could've split the corals... No one could pierce holes in the corals. They would make a priceless necklace, fit for a queen, if strung together, but the case was desperate and no one could not think of what was to be done."

Salam expressed her sympathy for the king, "What a pity... tch, tch..."

Aachi had come to the end of sweeping the street front and said, "Child, run in and get me the *kolam* flour[2], my darling..."

"I shall get it in a jiffy, but pause the story till I return," Salam cautioned her granny and, holding up her ankle - length petticoat with one hand, she ran into the house.

At this moment, Aachi saw Ekkimatan Pillai returning from somewhere in a hurry.

"Is it Matan Pillai? Has Bhomu delivered?" she enquired anxiously.

"Yes, she has delivered—a girl." His tone implied that the female child was an unwanted addition to the family, an uninvited guest.

"Why do you say it bitterly? You should be glad that what was in the belly emerged safely. What is the use of complaining? Can it change anything? Can a dog open the gate by barking?"

Ekkimatan Pillai went away, his head drooping.

Salam had brought the *kolam* powder and handed it to her grandmother. Aachi used it to draw artistic patterns just outside the threshold, which was slightly green with the coating of fresh cowdung.

"How did the king manage to thread the corals?" Asked Diravi trying to take the old woman back to the ancient times of her tale.

"Everyone had given it up as an impossible task. The king at last sent for the well known Chettiar, who had business relations with the palace, and said to him, 'Oh Chettiar, I do not care what you do. But bring these corals strung into a necklace in the morning or else you will lose your head. That is final.'

Salam was critical of the king. "What a cruel king! Poor fellow, the Chettiar. What could he do? The king was a cruel one, wasn't he, Aachi?"

Diravi was critical of Salam. "What do you know, poor ignorant girl? What the king says is law. And once he says something, it is final. Isn't it so?" asked Diravi. And then he added, "Aachi tell the story quickly. I hear Father coming. He will bawl us out if he finds us listening to stories instead of studying. Finish the tale before Father comes."

Aachi tried to be brief and paced up the narration. "Chettiar came home with the corals. He was in a fix, unable to think, or even move his limbs. He had two daughters called Thangamme and Thayamme, both virgins, both as beautiful as celestial damsels and very intelligent. Finding their father sorrowful, they asked him what the matter was. When they heard the tale, they asked for the corals. Taking the corals, they said, "Dont worry. Go to bed and sleep well. We'll do what has to be done." The two girls thought intensely and arrived at a clever solution to the problem. They kept the corals in a row near an ant-hill, after touching the ends of the corals with a needle dipped in jaggery water. They kept a thread dipped in jaggery water before the first coral in the series. In the morning, when they woke up and examined the corals, the ants had drilled a hole right through the corals and threaded them with the string dipped in jaggery water. The corals were thus pierced and strung together into a necklace.

"The Chettiar was overjoyed. Not only had he escaped with his life, but the wit of his daughters was also a matter of pride. Even before it was quite bright, he rushed to the king with the threaded corals. The king too was greatly impressed, his wonder knew no end. He enquired as to how it had been done. The proverb says that in bad times you have bad ideas; the Chettiar proudly told the king what his daughters Thangamme and Thayamme had done. Immediately, the king said, 'The place for such clever girls is not the house of a Chettiar, but the palace of the king. Give me your two daughters in marriage.'

Who could object to the words of the king? The Chettiar begged for a day's respite to arrange the wedding. And he came back in sadness and despair. If it were today, anyone would be pleased to give his daughters in marriage to a king. But in the old days, the restrictions and feelings of caste were strong. The Chettiars, in particular, could not think of marrying their daughters out of their caste. Even a king could not have the daughter of a self-respecting Chettiar for his bride, try how he might. 'How could the king insult me by asking for my daughters in marriage? What of my caste? What of the respect due to me? If a man, who cannot see, claims that he has seen paradise, should we ask him to describe it? Now the king has asked me for my daughters in marriage. If I refuse, he will have me killed and then force them into marriage with him. My family's name will be mud.'

The Chettiar came to a conclusion and asked his daughters to go and fetch some things from the basement. The poor girls did not know what had transpired in the palace and, suspecting nothing, they went into the basement. The Chettiar bade his men to seal the passage to the basement and then he too cast himself into its depths, so that he couldn't emerge. The whole family perished. But the virgins, who died for no fault of their own or of the Chettiar, cursed the king, and the city was a victim of famine, fevers, and earthquakes for a long time.

Some of the menfolk of the Chettiar families, fearing the anger of the king, escaped with their lives, braved the rain and the sun, jungle, and strange lands, and migrated a long way with their family deities, Singa Vinayaka and Nagaramma, and reached Eraniyal at long last, after great privation. A few other men went to Ottar, with their Desika Vinayaka of emerald leading them. They married into various castes and new castes multiplied. In the three streets of Eraniyal and in the other places, the Chettiars from Kaveripoompattinam became the Seven Towns' Chettiars. The name remains. The original Singa Vinayaka idol is in our temple at the end of the street. The goddess, Nagaramma, is a mile away in Oduparai," finished Aachi. From inside, rose the voice of the children's father, "Why do you waste time listening to the old woman's tales instead of reading your books, early in the morning?" He took his mother also to task, "How many times am I to tell you—allow the children to study in the mornings. Don't spoil them."

Diravi and his sister were sure that if they persisted in listening to stories, they might even be beaten. So, they signalled to their grandmother that they could continue listening to later developments at some other time and, opening their books, read the first lines their eyes fell on. But Diravi could not help but stop his reading to admire the old woman's artistry with *kolam* powder. His eyes were drawn to the superb brightness and skill of his grandmother's art.

Three

The morning sun was low in the east. Men hurried to the fields, women with brass pots were going to the river to fetch water, and people, after bathing, were on their way to the temple—the street was filling up with all kinds of people.

The house opposite her's was not awake to all this wealth of activity, as Unnamalai Aachi noted with great distaste. She could hear her brother bawling. Her brother was Koonangani Pillai. To Diravi, Koonangani Pillai Paatta[1].

"What women of misfortune fill this house! Not one of them has the sense of sensitivity to get up before dawn and sweep the street in front of the house, sprinkle cowdung -water on it, and draw the auspicious *kolam* before the man of the house gets up and leaves... My throat is dry talking to you all. How will our family prosper?"

The old man cleared his throat and spat. The sound reached Aachi in her house.

A little later, from Koonangani Paatta's house emerged his first wife, Ponamu Aachi, armed with a broom and bucket, muttering something to herself sleepily.

Ponamu Aachi looked older than Father, thought Diravi. An old woman—she was 50 years of age. Unlike Unnamalai

Aachi, she wore coloured clothes or the kind of clothes that did not emphasize her age. Otherwise, with her big earrings, and bare chest, she was like Aachi.

As soon as she saw Unnamalai Aachi, without betraying anything about her husband's shouts, she said, "You have already finished, sister-in-law? So soon? At least one morning, I want to get up before you and finish all this before you...bet it will never happen!"

For Diravi, to hear her talk like that was in itself irritating. She not only slept till sunrise, which was unbecoming in a woman, but was not even ashamed of it. Her tongue was seven cubits long.

"Who is it? Ponamu? Why don't you get up before me and sweep the street before I do; nobody prevents you. Isn't Ananji Pillai up yet? Why is Brother shouting so early in the morning?"

"It isn't yet time for Ananji to get up. And no one has to instruct your brother, my husband, to bawl me out and find fault with me. If he opens his mouth to Ananji, she will break him open and salt him… It is I and I alone who is going to walk away with all this as his heir..."

Diravi noticed Ponamu Aachi's tone and smiled mischievously in a knowing manner at his grandmother, who said, "You quarrel among yourselves. Why should I buy into the trouble?" She picked up the broom and bucket and went in. She washed the bucket, upended it in its corner, and left the broom leaning against the wall of the corner. Then, she went to the well.

All the cooking vessels were washed, and Kuttiamma had carried them into the kitchen, from which smoke billowed, indicating that the oven was lit. Unnamalai Aachi took a little of the ash, kept in the wooden receptacle, put it into her mouth and, holding it so between her teeth and lips, went down to the backyard.

Diravi and Salam vied with each other in reading aloud. They had finished and were about to go in, when a man of about 50 came to the front of the house and asked, "Children, is your father at home?" He sounded rather anxious.

"He is in the backyard and will presently be going to Kurunthankode. Shall I call him? Who shall I say calls?"

The man who had come showed some signs of overcoming his anxiety.

"Yes, boy. My master sent me...from Puthan Street…I am to tell your father that he has to go to your brother-in-law's house immediately..."

"Oh, Brother-in-law sent you! Who are you?"

"I work in your brother-in-law's shop."

"Oh, please wait. I shall call Father..."

He shouted "Father!" and ran into the house towards the backyard. Meanwhile, Kuttiamma too came out of her kitchen and enquired of the visitor what the matter was.

"I don't know anything about that, but he wanted me to fetch him immediately," repeated the messenger. Without knowing the reason, Kuttiamma was afraid that something was seriously wrong.

Diravi informed his father of the visitor from his brother-in-law's shop. Diravi was late for school and hurried through his cold bath. While he was drinking his morning gruel in the kitchen, his sister Nagammai's charming face flitted before his mind's eye.

"Nagammai Akka[2] is a year and a half older than I am. Her wedding took place only six months ago in this very house." His mother, father, and granny had corrected him many times, telling him that her husband's name was Sivananda Perumal Pillai and not Sevantha Perumal Pillai, but Diravi continued to think of him as only Sevantha Perumal Pillai.

"He lives in Puthan street; it is within calling distance."

But why should he send for Father at dawn today? Could Nagammai Akka have done something wrong? No; Akka is incapable of wrong-doing. It would be a sin to think of Nagammai doing any wrong. Pity... the poor girl is so innocent, she does not know enough to weep when beaten...Brother-in-law's mother is frightful to look at and frightening to think of...Aachi said her name was Papathi. Diravi was speaking to himself.

She wears only coloured saris...but her husband is not to be seen in the house...Brother-in-law's father was supposed to be dead. If he were dead, she too would wear only white. He stays in the market, never comes home.

All that apart, why should brother-in-law send for father just now? After the wedding, except for once, Nagammai Akka had never been to her father's house. Her mother-in-law had a cruel cat-like face.

After his morning meal, Diravi changed his shirt and dhoti. When he came out, he found that his father had not eaten his gruel, had abandoned the idea of going to Kurunthankode and had gone to Puthan Street instead.

The servant from Brother-in-law's shop was gossiping with Unnamalai Aachi. The old woman was enquiring into his parentage and assuring him that he was distantly related to her. "All Chettis are related," she told him. "In eight ways, they are related, but all the eight ways are evil," she quoted a proverb at him.

Diravi was irritated that his grandmother was gossiping with such a worthless fellow.

Salam was a student of the fifth grade. She gathered her friends from the same street, and called out loudly, "I am going to school."

Aachi immediately said, "You are a senseless girl. How many times have I told you that you should say 'I go now; will be back later', instead of saying 'I'm going to school'? It is inauspicious to say 'I go' without adding the word 'come'. It was only after Salai and said, "I go now and shall return," so that she was allowed to leave.

Diravi was a student of the 10th grade and his departure to school was accordingly sober. Aachi admonished him, "On the way to school, look into the Puthan Street house, your Akka's house. See what is happening...Anything might be happening," she added apprehensively.

"Yes, yes. I shall...I go and shall return," he shouted, taking his books and running out of the house.

No matter what the hurry, ingrained in him was the habit of looking for the right and auspicious omen, before stepping into the street. This was Aachi's strict order.

While he was waiting, the head-shaking old woman came with a pot of kitchen refuse on her head, saying, "Darling, wait for the proper omen. I am a widow; don't set off looking me in the face."

The next fellow to pass by was a wood chopper. If he set off for the day on sighting him, Diravi knew he would acquire a wound that bled.

The third person to come was Ammalu with an empty pot balanced at her waist.

Lastly came the fishwife with a load of fish on her head. "Ah, good omen boy!" said Aachi, who was also looking out.

Diravi stepped into the street and hurried along.

"I am late. The school bell must have rung. If I go to Akka's house now, it will be much too late for school… But I should go and see why Brother-in-law sent for Father so early…I am anxious to know. I shall go and see for myself and then go to school." He walked as fast as his legs could carry him.

Four

When he arrived at Nagu Akka's husband's house, Diravi felt as if events of great consequence had taken place. The neighbourhood had collected in front of the house, and some even stood inside.

Father sat sorrowfully in the front verandah of the house. Two relatives of Brother-in-law were whispering something into Father's ears. Brother-in-law was sitting a little farther away with a sorrowful expression. He breathed irregularly with unexpressed emotion.

Inside, in the kitchen, Nagu was lying on her stomach, sobbing, her shoulders rising and falling. When she saw Diravi in the kitchen, she wept even harder.

She—Papathi it was—was shouting at Sister: "Why do you lie on your stomach and weep and wail? Are we murdering you? Are we beating or hurting you? You have been in this house for some months—did you want for anything? I don't know. I ask you… You looked starved when you entered this house. Now you are twice of what you were. You have put on weight. You became a woman after you came here. What games did you not play in the house? I told you a hundred times, to behave properly. Don't play such games.

A dog would be more respected than I was in this house. Did my crack of a son at least listen to me? If it had been any one else, he would have immediately put you out of the house and closed the door on you. He, poor innocent fellow, waited six months, six long months…Who knows what sin you committed in your last birth? As a result of that sin you are this way now..."

The old woman went on endlessly; Diravi was hard put to make any sense of it…Why? What was wrong with his sister? Was she blind, or lame, or deaf? He could not get anything out of the old woman's throaty mutterings.

Diravi came out on to the verandah. He recollected the fellows who were still muttering to his father. One was Ekki Matan Pillai who had that very morning, before dawn, been talking to Aachi; the other was Saastha Pillai who often borrowed money from Father. The rest of them were people of the neighbourhood. Had they come to mediate and do justice?

Ekki Matan Pillai said to Diravi's father, "Nagaru Pillai, listen; a quarrel in the street is always cooling to others' eyes. Why say this or that and make things public? Each one will add his own words and ideas. No one needs to know anything; let us keep it secret. Take Nagammai home…we shall talk later."

Ekki Matan Pillai spoke nicely. Father was bewildered by all this loaded talk; it was obvious.

"Why should I? It has been only six months since the wedding was celebrated. If he now says that he doesn't want the girl, should I take her back? Is this a town where no one cares for justice? Will no one listen to the injustice of it? To do harm to a woman is a great sin; it will not go unrequited; evil, great evil, will befall the person who harms a woman."

Father was waxing angrier by the moment.

Brother-in-law spoke measured words as if he had said all he had to say, like a great lawyer.

"I have no big revelations to make. I take this round about way of revealing the matter to you, because I don't want to commit the great sin of harming a woman. Take her to a lady doctor and have her examined. But even that I don't want to say. Just take her away from here—that is all I ask..."

Saying that he didn't want to say anything, he said things of great import—clever fellow... Heaven knew if he knew what exactly he was saying.

Father's face was set, and anger leapt visibly from his eyes and brows. There was nothing he could do or understand. And if he were any more late for school, his master might take him to task.

Diravi went down the street, into the shortcut shaded path lined with fig trees, over which the wind rustled. Brown as well as young leaves came floating down. Two or three years ago he would have put a young fig leaf in his ear in his superstitious belief that it would prevent him from feeling the sharp cuts of the teacher's cane on arriving late, his arithmetic homework incomplete, but now he was wiser; he knew that the tender fig leaf in the ear did not help the pain; he would have to bear it as best he might.

But the bell had rung just then. Nothing untoward happened. He was not late.

He sat in his place on the bench, but did not feel like talking to any of his mates. His mind was full of a thousand things which he failed to fully understand; they were dancing in wild confusion.

The first period was an English lesson. Inji[2] Kolappa Pillai was busy teaching the prescribed lesson; none of it registered with Diravi.

Why should Thangamme and Thayamme die, instead of marrying the king and living happily thereafter?

This evil woman, Papathi, and her son, Sevantha Perumal, my brother-in-law—why should they insist that my father take Nagu Akka back home?

What a pity! Nagu's face was red due to weeping—red like the hibiscus. Will she die of sorrow and weeping?

But this was wrong of Brother-in-law.

Though a moneyed man, no one had given Sevantha Perumal a girl in marriage till he was 35. Why? Was it because of his father? No, certainly not. Kannu Pillai, the father was a sick man. His face was swollen with some disease. His fingers were contracted, wrinkled, and always dirty. Saying it was contagious, his wife Papathi, had driven him away from home. That house, that shop, and all that they had, had been his property. He was living with the Krishna woman[3], his mistress. She cooked and cared for him in his ill-health, while his wife and his son had driven him out of his own house…at least, the Krishna woman was kind.

The second period was an arithmetic lesson. The teacher had not turned up that day, long might he live! The biology teacher arrived, drew a plant on the board, asked the class to copy it and was then lost in a book he carried. Diravi was free to think his own thoughts, untrammelled by any necessity to attend to what was being said.

Pity it was… Would Father have taken Akka home? What would now happen to Akka?

Can she be married again to someone else?

The eldest of his sisters, she had been named after Aachi Unnamalai; her wedding had taken place a few years ago in Pazhavadai. I don't remember all the details of that wedding now… But Nagu Akka's wedding was only six months ago…I remember it, as if it had happened yesterday.

In the beginning, it was Papathi who broached the subject in the temple to Aachi. I was standing nearby when she spoke. "Oh, Unnamalai sister… Aren't you looking for a bridegroom for your granddaughter Nagammai? Your virgins' quarters are full." And Unnamalai Aachi said, "What to do Papathi? We haven't yet cleared the debts incurred at the wedding of our eldest, Unnamalai. We had to sell a little of the Kurunthankode lands for that wedding. What is left produces enough for us to eat; so, Dorai is reduced to taking on other people's lands to cultivate…Who is there to help Dorai? He has to stand alone Somehow, the wheels have to turn. Otherwise, how can we undertake this wedding now?" Unnamalai Aachi lamented.

"Why think of all that and weep? Am I not your close relative? Should I not help? My son Mookan is unmarried.

In what way is he defective? Now he runs the shop without anyone's assistance…I should see his wedding celebrated in good time"

Papathi used to call her son (brother-in-law Sevantha Perumal) Mookan. Suddenly, Papathi looked round and, lowering her voice, whispered into my Aachi's ears—I could hear her, I have snake's ears.

"Why seek a groom elsewhere? Aren't we all related and don't we all know each other well. Choose a good day and send someone for the horoscope[4]—I shall give you Mookan's horoscope. If his horoscope agrees with Nagammai's, we can celebrate the wedding immediately. You do what you can by way of groom price and dowry and wedding expenses. Let it all be in the family. Let us not allow talk of it to get out among our evil-minded neighbours. It's getting late. Let me take leave of you."

Aachi was impressed. She dragged me home—she was in such a hurry to get home and talk about it with her daughter-in-law and son.

It was time to light the lamps. "Eh, Kuttiamma," she began and told her all the things that Papathi said, skilfully mimicking her very tones. Mother too was impressed. "But he is the son of a man who has some unknown disease. And Papathi too is a woman to be feared. She and her son drove her husband from his home and took possession of his property. She is to be feared; she is evil."

Aachi too was of the same mind about Papathi and the father's disease. But it was marriage into a rich family. "And one should not neglect prosperity when it is offered. "We should not kick it away," she counselled.

When Father returned from the fields; his mother and wife took turns hurrying to tell him of the offer. He was not willing to believe it. It was beyond his expectations.

"But she is a bad woman, not to be trusted. Her words may be sweet, but her actions will bring bitterness. After the wedding, she might take it into her head to demand this and that. How can we give her anything without the wherewithal for it. The boy's father suffers from an incurable disease. How can we be sure that the son also will not suffer from it? That is why he's still single, though he is rich."

Then, Unnamalai Aachi's brother, Koonangani Pillai Paatta came in. When he heard of the offer, he said, "Eh, Nagaru Pillai! Don't think of this thing and that and get into a state. Our girl should live happily with enough to put into her belly, with a good young husband for many years. If you hesitate and ask why nobody has given him a girl in marriage so far, your problem will not be solved. You have married off your first daughter; she lives in poverty. For your financial position, you cannot find anyone better than a daily wage earner who works in the temple. If *he* falls ill, the kitchen will fall silent and the cat will occupy the oven; there will be nothing in the house to eat."

Listening to Paatta's advice, everyone was convinced that it was the right thing to do.

"Other weddings are fixed for the day after tomorrow; so, it must be a good day. What day is today?" Paatta asked.

"Today is Monday. Wednesday is really auspicious," said Aachi, smiling happily.

"Yes, it is good. Day after tomorrow, I shall go to Papathi and get the horoscope, and go to Thengappattinam to consult the astrologer. If the horoscopes agree, let the marriage take place. The wedding garland might be waiting for Nagammai in this place, who can say?" said grandfather and went his way.

Koonangani Paatta was ten years older than Unnamalai Aachi. He was 70. But how healthy he was! There was not a single hair on his head, but his skin glowed like sandalwood, clear as the colour of turmeric. His limbs were long and straight. I liked Koonangani Paatta very much.

Nagammai Akka was standing in the dark, listening shyly to all this, and shaking; I laughed when I spied her standing in the dark.

"Is Nagammai Akka..."

The bell rang. The next period was the Tamil class. Govinda Rama Iyer took over. If you were inattentive, you would get a taste of his cane, which was ever ready in his hand. Diravi tried to stay his thoughts and turned to his lesson.

Five

At noon, as soon as the intermission bell rang, Diravi ran home.

What was happening in the house? Had father brought Nagu Akka home?

As soon as he turned a corner, a black cat crossed his path. What a bad omen! He turned thrice around where he stood to ward off the effects of the ill omen and walked further into his street.

Ekki Aachi's calf lay on the road, the rope around its neck trailing across the street. He was about to put his foot across it, when he remembered his Aachi saying that it was a bad omen to step over the rope of a tethered cow or calf. He got over it by stepping on the rope with both feet, touching the calf and raising his fingers to his eyes before going on.

When he arrived home, Diravi found his house crowded with neighbours, both men and women. It was all crowd and confusion.

Koonangani Paatta was saying something loudly. The neighbour on the other side, Annamalai Pillai, was also saying something at equal volume. Listening to them, Father was holding his head in his hands silently, with his eyes closed.

Inside, in the verandah of the courtyard, Nagu Akka lay like she had lain in her husband's house, on her stomach. Mother, grandmother and other women gathered round her, trying to pacify her and make her stop sobbing.

As soon as she saw Diravi, Ponamu Aachi began.

"Look here boy, look at what your brother-in-law has done. Have you ever seen a fellow like him? The girl is like a bouquet, like clear water. Six months after the wedding, 'I don't like the girl. Take her back,' the fellow says, the crack-brain, and your father brings his daughter back home... What a thing to do!" She spoke, emphasising what she said by clapping one palm against the other, laying a finger along her nose and resting an elbow on her other palm, each gesture emphasised by a loud exclamation of disbelief.

Koonangani Paatta's second wife, Ananji Pillai Aachi, interrupted her. "Diravi is a little fellow. What does he know about things around him? You talk, as if he were a grown person."

"Eh, Diravi, you have to go back to school in the afternoon. In this confusion, nothing has been cooked in the house. Come inside. I shall give you the cold rice left over from the morning. Eat it and go back to school," said Unnamalai Aachi, respecting a young boy's hunger. He followed her.

Unless he talked to Aachi in detail, he would never get to know what had really happened. But Aachi was upset and angry. She would not be able to tell him anything in a cogent way. He badly wanted to question her, but he suppressed that desire for the time being. Aachi served the cold rice on a metal plate and gave him tender mango pickle to go with it, all the while expressing her anger, anxiety and irritation in an endless flow of words.

Salam had never seen such an upset situation before. It was all new to her, but she wasn't around. She might have gone to school already, thought Diravi.

When Diravi had rinsed his hands and come out, Annamalai Pillai was telling his father, "Oh, Nagaru Pillai, don't lose heart at what these hopeless fellows have done. We have village trustees and elders in our families; let us see what they can do. The wedding did not take place secretly, without announcements. We paid the village trustees and elders their dues and celebrated the wedding in their presence. I told the Society President, Velu Pillai. He told me that I was to come with you and meet him in the evening. He has also asked Sevantha Perumal to come at the same time…All the trustees of our community will be present. Let us talk things through. If necessary, we shall call a community of nobodies? When he asks, he should be married to the girl, now when he does not want her, we should take her back! Is this justice? Can a marriage be dissolved this easily? A marriage is for a thousand years, forever! Can it be broken off like this? We shall see…" He challenged those present to offer objections to his observations.

If he stopped to listen any further, he would be late for school, Diravi told Aachi and stepped down into the street towards school.

The midday sun burned like fire. But Diravi did not feel the heat. All sorts of things were tearing his mind apart—as if it were a dung-heap on which a donkey had rolled for comfort.

So, tonight, at President Velu Pillai's house, there would be a heated debate. Brother-in-law and his men would be present...but there would be much confusion.

It was Nagu Akka's singular misfortune that all this had happened to her. In Unnamalai Akka's house there was no trouble. That brother-in-law was a nice, decent fellow. Hmm—that Wednesday. I remember all that happened that day as if it were only yesterday.

Early in the morning Paatta came in hastily and called Father, Mother and Paatti together. He drew a palm-leaf from the folds of his waist cloth, wrapped in a piece of paper.

"Eh, Nagaru Pillai, this is the horoscope of Sevantha Pillai. Take it and keep it safe. Keep Nagu's horoscope ready. You have already written to your elder son-in-law, haven't you? I shall come in the evening. We'll go to Pazhavadai, take the eldest son-in-law of the family, go together to Thengappattinam and consult the astrologer. Everything will depend on that. Let us see if the horoscopes match. If everything goes off without any hitch, we shall break five coconuts[1] in the Vinayaka temple."

While Paatta was saying all this, in the inner room in the smoke-darkened corner near which the calendar hung, a lizard screeched.

Hearing the lizard, Paatta was overcome with joy.

"See Unnamalai—this wedding will certainly occur; the lizard is the voice of God. Oh Singa Vinayaka! When this wedding is over, I shall break not just five coconuts, I shall arrange a whole festival for you." He closed his eyes and prayed for a moment to Singa Vinayaka and only after that did he go home. At this point, Mother, Father and Paatti were unable to move hand or foot. In such a hurry, were they to do everything at once? Father rushed to Kurunthankode, did all that was necessary, and then hurried back. Aachi, who often went to see Nagu Akka, asked her with great solicitude, "Have you bathed? Have you eaten?" This was her way of showing her love for her granddaughter, who was waiting to be married.

Even this young girl, Salam, I remember, was caught by the spirit of joy and was running hither and thither.

Till he got to school, into class, and was seated in his place on the bench, Diravi was, as if stunned by some blow, unable to think of anything else.

His bench-mate, Ambalavanam asked him, "Why are you not your usual self? Is it true that your brother-in-law has sent your sister back to your home, discarded her?" Diravi was irritated beyond measure.

"Oh, it is not so easy to cast aside a wife. He can't do it. If he does, he will go like this." Diravi demonstrated how he would go if he did that unspeakable thing in the manner peculiar to people of that region. He meant that Nagu's husband would be menacled and taken to jail.

As the bell rang just then, no one else said anything. All talk ceased. It was time for the science class. Krishna

Panicker was teaching in his usual earnest way. Diravi could not grasp anything of what he was saying. His mind was full of thoughts about Nagu Akka; of the memories of what had happened that day and later, at the wedding.

The poor girl had been full of joy throughout that day, thinking of her wedding. The dark corner just beyond the door was her usual place. Only when there were no men about the house, would she go to the courtyard, backyard or elsewhere; at no time, since she came of age, was she allowed to come out of the house into broad daylight. A virgin was not expected to show herself before any men.

Poor girl. How could she spend her time sitting in a dark corner? If she peeped out, it was enough to set Mother bawling aloud.

"Why do you peep out and show yourself. Virgins should lie in their corner and not show themselves."

How long could she have continued like this? Only after she got married, could she step out of her dark corner. How did it matter what kind of a husband he was? "He" meant freedom from that dark corner to which she was confined. So she must have thought! But what freedom did she finally get? Poor girl.

When I returned home after school I learnt that Paatta and Father had left for Pazhavadai. Aachi also told me that they were going to take the elder son-in-law with them to Thangappattinam and see the astrologer, compare the horoscopes and return only after that.

Mother and Aachi, would not cease talking about it. Every 10 or 15 minutes, Aachi would go out to see whether she could spot Father returning.

"For the elder daughter, Unnamalai, remember how many horoscopes we checked? In one, Saturn was too powerful; in another, it was Mars. It was the third day or what not. How many times and to how many astrologers did we go? We are looking at Nagu's horoscope only now... If the horoscopes agree by the grace of our Nagaru Goddess, then..."

Aachi who must have said this a thousand times to Mother, said it again. Wouldn't Mother be tired of hearing this? But no, she was not.

"We brought them up with great care and pain. If only we could marry them off, so that they can be happy and live dry-eyed, our job is done. We want them to be happy and lead good lives," said Mother as often.

"But these are the unfortunate ones. Why should they suffer so? If my father was alive, would they be like this? What he said was law in Thiruvithankode. The eldest son, Mookandi Pillai, was a name to contend with. The house would always be crowded with relatives and friends. If diamonds were to be examined, if gold was to be estimated, his word was the last—there was no further appeal. He was the expert. The house was filled with the perfume of jackfruit—there was always a roomful of it. We stored palm-sugar in the granary; there was no scarcity of paddy or of coconut. The arecanut bunches gathered from the gardens were stored in water. In the backyard stood five cows…not cows like the ones we see today, all skin and bone—each cow was like an elephant. If all that wealth were ours today would these girls be wed like this?"

I could not stand it any longer. "Why? What happened to all that? Did the crow fly away with it all?" I remember having asked.

"What are you babbling about? The crow did not fly away with it, nor did the cat eat it all. It was all spent by that brother of mine, Koonangani—he ran through all of it in no time. With and without his father's knowledge, he spent it all on cheap women. His father made a fortune eating frugally, enjoying himself moderately, always careful about money. But in what way is he better now, this brother of mine? The proverb says that the man with two wives is to be pitied—how true—we too became daily-wage-earners… your fate was this…"

This was her usual burden of songs and sayings. Whatever the occasion, if Aachi began talking about the wealth of her father's house, she always went on like this. When Aachi was a young girl, a lady teacher had come in a bullock-cart to tutor her. She was brought up as their darling by her father and grandfather. At last, she was married with pomp. Diraviam Pillai was her husband's name… She could go on endlessly, but when she came to the name of her husband she would stop; she was not supposed to say his name out loud. I was named after him. If she called me by my name, she would be committing a sacrilege; so, instead, she would call me “Kannu darling”. Kannu almost became my name.

But what a grasshopper mind have I! I was thinking of Nagu Akka and her trouble. When did it lose its way and stray into other paths, thinking of other things?

It was 9 at night when they came—I was waiting up for them. Salam was sleeping. Father and Paatta came in all asking, “It was all auspicious, eh?” and Paatta replied, “Yes, everything is auspicious. The horoscopes agree quite well.” Granny breathed a great sigh of relief, “Appa!”

Father too expressed his happiness.

“The astrologer was emphatic. ‘Two horoscopes agreeing to such a degree is rare. I have never seen two more suitable horoscopes’, he said in so many words.”

Mother was anxious about another thing. “Children, what do the horoscopes say about their having children?” she asked.

It was Paatta who replied first. “Both horoscopes bear the mark of that good fate, to have children. There will be five boys and four girls from this marriage,” he said.

Everyone was happy and Aachi said, “The horoscopes agree. Now other things have to follow. Tomorrow, tell Papathi that the horoscopes agree. If she wants to consult any astrologer, let her; ask her to. Then we should get together and talk about what is to be done at the wedding. Now, the community is not what it used to be; someone might say something or the other in opposition. We should be careful. If the right persons try, even stone can dissolve in water.”

"Paatta should talk it over with her," said Father. "You tell Papathi tomorrow that the horoscopes agree. Then talk about what should be done."

Father lowered his voice and continued, "Ask her what she expects from us? Our status is known. So, enquire of her what she expects; ask her nicely. Then we can talk about other things." The night was full of talk of the wedding to be.

Six

"Eh, Diraviam. Did you eat too well?" The voice was loud and clear. The sound of laughter followed. It was Krishna Panicker trying to rein in his fancies which were running away with him…

Diravi stood up and looked at his class without understanding what the laughter was about. "No Sir…I do not feel very well." He tried to say something more to retrieve the situation.

"All right. All right. Attend to the lesson," said Krishna Panicker and began to dictate notes. Diravi opened his notebook and tried to concentrate on the lesson.

At length, the bell rang and Krishna Panicker left. Next was the history class.

Wearing a dark green sari and blouse, teacher Elizabeth John walked in with beautifully measured steps, dancing and mincing her way into class. No student was afraid of her. She would begin dictating notes as soon as she came into class, reading from a book she carried. Everyone would have to take down what she read out. She did not teach. "Take down the notes clearly. Go home, read them and memorise them," were her instructions.

Without attending to what was being said, Diravi had cultivated the art of taking down what was said. His mind was free to roam where it would. But his thoughts were all of poor Nagu Akka. The day after they came back from the astrologer, Paatta went to Puthan Street, to Papathi's house and gave her to understand that the horoscopes matched well. The old woman did not trust even her closest relatives.

She said, "Yes, I understand. But anyhow, I shall ask my brother in Midalam, Odayan Pillai, to study the horoscopes of Mookan and Nagammai; he knows astrology very well; he is an expert. Nothing that he has said so far has gone wrong."

Paatta himself took the horoscopes to Papathis's brother. Two days later Odayan Pillai came to the house.

"The horoscopes agree ideally. After this marriage both families will prosper." So saying he laughed. Before he left he asked Unnamalai Aachi to come with him to Puthan Street to see Papathi. Aachi took me with her. Papathi whispered in Aachi's ears—I could however hear her; "Sister, it is all right. I have seen a girl when she was very young. After she matured, I haven't seen her… Mookan too wants to see her before he ties the thali round her neck. What shall I tell him?"

Aachi did not like that talk at all. "What are you saying? Have we become so progressive? In our community, no bridegroom has seen his bride before the wedding. Did our grooms see us before we married? In what way did we suffer because of that? I don't know, that is why I ask. Please tell me…" Papathi looked coolly at Aachi and said, "Not that I approve, sister…but times are changing." Aachi was furious.

"How are these days different? Do crows fly wrong side up these days? Do sheep and cows walk on two feet now? It is these men that are becoming different. What can the times do for that?"

"In the city of Thiruvananthapuram, girls of our community—when they go to school or to the cinema, are seen by the boys who are going to marry them. The boys stand in corners gazing boldly at the girls who pass." Papathi said, smugly.

"What is the use of all this foolish talk? It takes all sorts to make the world. Everywhere, there are those who have no history, no background, no family pride. If Mookan says something ignorant, you should not have encouraged him. *My daughters should not be looked at even by the king* was the principle on which the forefather of our community of Chettis buried his daughters alive. We come of that tradition and family. Now, Chettis are fallen on evil days. Why don't you think for yourself about what will happen. If Mookan comes and sees the girl and then says he does not like her, that he won't marry her, what will happen? Who will wed the virgin after that? That is why I say that it should not be. After she came of age, she has never stepped out into the daylight. Don't think I speak highly of her because she is my granddaughter. There is no defect in the girl—with sharp nose and charming eyes, she is as beautiful as water..."

Aachi spoke much, and fast, and stopped Papathi's talk. After that, she did not say that her son should see the girl before marriage.

But that was not the end of the matter. Before a wedding takes place, many things have to be done.

What can you give for dowry? What wedding gifts? Jewels worth how much? The wedding expenses should all be borne by the girl's family."

Papathi added one thing after another.

At last, Father, accompanied by his elder son-in-law and Paatta, went for a final discussion with her. I accompanied them.

Paatta began, "Papathi, you know full well the status of Nagaru Pillai. If you ask for an elephant and a howdah, where will he get them? This wedding will take place, I tell you. Tell us briefly what you have in mind."

Papathi began in good order, "Why, brother, do you talk like this? What defect do you find in Mookan? By God's grace, there is no lack of wealth or health. He earns well now. I have no other son. Tomorrow, all this will be his. To whom else will it all go? My days are almost over. Then, your girl is going to enjoy all this. There are persons who promise him 20,000 rupees or even 30,000. But I have to consider all things. Money is not the only thing; life should be sweet and pleasant. If you offer less money, I don't mind—I only want that he should marry into a family that is…"

She kept talking without committing herself to anything. She spoke as if the fathers of all the eligible girls were offering their daughters to her son, as if they were standing in a queue. She forgot that because he was the son of a diseased man, Mookan was single even at 35.

Little by little, the cat came out of the bag.

"Why do I haggle like this, making me scream till my voice is hoarse? Whatever you do, it is going to be for your daughter. Tomorrow, she is going to be the lady of this house, lording over it all. Give her a dowry, some old lands which will yield five kottais[1] of paddy to feed the family. Make 30 sovereigns worth of gold jewels, and give some two thousand rupees in cash. That is all. But you should foot the expenses of the wedding. Vessels for domestic use, enough sweets to distribute among the townsfolk on milk, fruits, and other things—you know…the usual. You should do enough, so that no one might have cause to feel that things were not sufficiently well done nor given—that is all I ask. I have no other son, you see; he is the only one. If I miss this chance, I cannot celebrate a second wedding."

Paatta lost his patience.

"Why do you say all this, betraying yourself? Do you think we don't know anything? They will do what they did for their eldest girl. Can we put it down in writing? But what you ask is too much, as you yourself know very well. The land you ask for will cost 5,000; 30 sovereigns will mean atleast three thousand rupees cash, two thousand… other things will need at least three thousand rupees more. If you add it all up, it comes to 13,000 rupees. Then sweets, feeding of guests, and new clothes will come to two or three thousand. If an elephant begins to bring forth lambs what will happen? He has another daughter to marry, a boy to educate, remember. So, all your demands are too much for him; he will do as much as he did for his first daughter. No more." Papathi saw that Paatta was serious and asked.

"Tell me plainly, how much you can give, without any more ado?"

Father said, "I can give land to yield four kottais from my Kurunthankode lands and two thousand rupees. I shall give the cash, you buy whatever you want. As for our expenses towards the marriage and for feeding the guests from the girl's side, we can give you five hundred rupees. All this comes to six thousand and five hundred rupees. Over and above this, clothes, presents, and other things would cost me something like another one thousand five hundred."

Papathi haggled about it all. Land, 2,000 rupees for purchases, another thousand rupees cash. The wedding should be done at our expense in our house—everything was agreed on, at last.

"It is a little above what I can afford. What can I do? But I want my girl to marry into a rich family and be happy. I am a dried tile—I do not stand to lose anything..." said Father going back home with his elder son-in-law, my Paatta and me.

Then things occurred rather rapidly. They went to the astrologer again and fixed the date for erecting the wedding pandal, for melting the gold to fashion the thali[2] in Puthan Street at the groom's house. All this was fixed for the same day, the first Sunday in the latter half of May.

Father himself wrote out the invitations that were auspiciously marked with turmeric powder and sent them east and west. On Friday, the women of the house, Unnamalai

Aachi, the daughter of Ananji Pillai Aachi, Aunt Thayee who married into the family at the corner street, and others went round the village. I went along to invite the men.

Aunt Thayee arrived in her wedding sari, making a rustling sound. Unnamalai Akka was not able to wear her silk sari properly and, to my great amusement, she had tied it up somewhat incoherently. All the children enjoyed the wedding preparations… Watching all this, the "head-shaking old woman" most fittingly observed, "When Chettis fall on evil days, they wear silk."

Ponamu Aachi, who overheard this chided the "head-shaking old woman." "Why do you misquote the proverb which says that Chettis will wear silk even in evil days?"

Everything was noisy and confused, Unnamalai Akka was placing the kumkum[3] mark on her forehead and rubbing it off to improve it. Unnamalai Aachi was waxing angry.

"Before the Chetti starts, it will be the end of the city," she said. "You are all properly dressed. Don't waste time like this; invite all the people of the town. You boy, yours is the responsibility to tell the men to come to the wedding. Don't forget any of them."

At last, we all moved towards the street and were about to step out, when Aachi called out, "They are going to invite the townsfolk. Why do you stand by silently; make the appropriate sounds; sing kolava[4], which is considered auspicious.

Everyone made the appropriate "kola kola" sounds, with fists held to their mouths, and it was enough to make my ears ring. I was afraid I'd go deaf with all that noise.

"Watch the omen before you step into the street. Eh Salam, have you checked your hair with flowers. Step out into the street and walk back from the next house so that you make the right omen for these people setting out to invite the town," ordered Unnamalai Aachi. Salam, shy with so many eyes on her, and in her hurry, holding up her slipping petticoat with one hand, walked to and back again from the next house to provide the right omen. Aachi hurried us into the street saying, "Start, start." Sister and Aunt walked surrounded by the whisper of silks, and I walked into the street with the gait of a king. It was all quite eventful!

We went to one house after another, inviting everyone for the wedding. "On Sunday, at 8 o'clock, and before 10 is the final *nichyathamboolam*.[5] At the same time is the erection of the first pillar[6] of the wedding pandal. You should all come."

When Aunt or Sister said this, I also echoed their words, adding, "Ask the men of the house also to come." And they teased me with, "Ah, this is the bride's brother. Look how proud he is."

It was the same story, at house after house. I was sweating with the effort of it all. How many times was one to repeat the same thing over and over again? Tired, I began to make mistakes. All the women laughed at me, indulgently.

Meanwhile, the bridegroom's party had also sent out two girls and a boy like me, to tell the town that they were melting the gold for the thali at the same hour. The two parties met halfway, it was all good fun.

Seven

As soon as the bell rang, the teacher, Elizabeth John minced her way out as delicately as she had entered. The next period was arithmetic. The teacher had lately been afflicted with paralysis and had not come to school at all for many days. For 45 minutes, the students were free to enjoy themselves as they wanted.

A few students went out of the class and played the parrot-cage game beneath the tamarind tree. Some played the one-leg-lame game. Some others urged Diravi to join them in kabaddi[1], though he was not inclined to.

Like a forest river, his thoughts were running riot within. When his mind was racing with thoughts, how could he play?

Everything connected with the wedding had proceeded with due joy and order. Was it all for this pitiable conclusion?

On the morning of the *nichyathamboolam*, how joyous had it all been! Clad in a new dress, Vembu Iyer was making a mountain of idlis. Koonangani Paatta was ordering him about.

Guests from the town and from outside places filled the house.

Only Ponamu Aachi's daughter, Neelapillai Aunt, had refused to come. "Why should I, a widow, come to a wedding?" she asked and stayed away. But her son, Chidambaram, was very much in evidence running hither and thither. Koonangani Paatta's two wives, Ponamu Aachi and Ananji Pillai Aachi were talking loudly, and frequent laughter of Ananji Pillai Aachi's daughter, Thayee Aunt, could be heard. Her husband, Kolappa Uncle, was sitting on a carpet spread in the courtyard, talking loudly to the guests.

Dum, Dum… Pi, Pi, Pi, sounded the *nadaswaram*. Women's loud gossip. The children's occasional shouts and whimpers—all sorts of noises were heard.

At the same time, the groom's family sent a party of 20 men and women following Kolammai, the sister-in-law, sister at one removed to the bridegroom, carrying a plate of plantain fruits, kumkum holder, sandal, garland, yellow towel, comb, mirror, and other beautiful things.

Kolammai placed the plate carefully on the floor of the mirror room, as it is called. To give her a plate in exchange, Mother and Unnamalai Akka made arrangements. In the mirror room, the inner room adjacent to the courtyard, was the kingdom of women; what they said was law.

"Mmm. Where is the bride? Should she be hiding today also?" asked Kolammai.

The inner room was opened and, from the dark interior, emerged Nagu Akka from her hiding place. She was dressed in new silks and adorned in all manners of unusual ways.

She was led into the group of women by Mother's mother who had come from Padmanabhapuram. Nagu Akka was named after that grandmother.

Oh, Nagu was shaking pitifully with fear and trying to withdraw into herself shyly. She was perspiring from head to toe and trying to keep her eyes fixed on the ground, with her head bent low.

The tall lamp was lit. Before it, on the plantain leaf was placed the Pillayar[2] made of cowdung.

Kolammai took the kumkum from the container she had brought and using the excuse of marking the bride's forehead with kumkum she raised Nagu Akka's chin to see how she looked. But Nagu Akka is a beautiful girl. Who could find fault with her face?

"Eh Kolammai. Peel the fruits you've brought and feed your in-laws," said someone and everybody laughed. Then she took a fruit from the plate, peeled it and without minding sister's objection said, "You should eat a little, the fruit has come from the house of your future husband," she forced a little of it into Nagu Akka's mouth.

In the courtyard and on the verandah's, men assembled in great numbers. Grandfather Padmanabhapuram Subbu Pillai, Mother's father, said loudly, "Read what is written." The time and the details of the wedding were written down and read aloud by Thanu Asan, the astrologer, for all to hear. The wedding was to be in 15 days' time.

As soon as it was read, women raised their voices in *kolavai*.

"Pay the money before the auspicious moment passes," said Mother's brother, Pandaram Pillai, who had come from Kulachal. Since the groom's father was absent, Papathi's sister's husband, the groom's uncle, called Thanu Pillai, came forward, took the towel off his shoulders and made a turban of it around his head. He advanced towards the tall lamp, and sat facing the east on the wooden seat readied for that purpose. Father bowed to the light, tucked 500 rupees in a roll of betel leaves, placed it on a silver plate and held it out to Thanu Pillai. He, in turn, stood up, bowed to the light, took the money and the betel leaves and tied it in the folds of his dhoti.

Then, the first pandal pillar was brought in. It was adorned with a paste of turmeric, garlanded and marked with big round spots of kumkum. It was kept ready and elder son-in-law and Ponamu Aachi's first son, Malu Pillai Uncle, carried it in, dug a hole in the south-west corner of the courtyard, and facing the east, set the pillar in it.

The women were ever ready to make the *kolavai*... the *kolavai* sound is something special. Everyone joined in the ululation three times, so that it sounded like a long, deep howl.

The first pillar for the pandal was set up. "Now we have to make the platform ready for the wedding ceremony," said Thayee Aunt's husband, Kolappa Pillai. Two or three bricks were spread in the centre of the courtyard, sandal paste applied to them liberally, and garlands placed on them. Kumkum spots were also put on them. The wedding platform was also ready now. Then Ponamu Aachi's younger son, Picha Pillai Uncle and Ananji Pillai's son, Andi Pillai Uncle distributed betel leaves and nuts among those present.

Then came the ceremony of eating, the grandest item on the programme. If anyone from the groom's house was neglected in this ceremony, there would be great agitation. Everyone was called individually seated, and idli, vadai, sweets, fruits, vegetables and other things served on plantain leaves.

"We shall have to hurry. Now we have to go to the groom's house and participate in the melting of the gold for the thali. It is already nine. Hurry," said someone from the bridegroom's side. All the groom's people prepared to go along with them as representatives of thebride's house, father, Paatta, uncle, elder brother-in-law and myself—altogether eight or nine persons set off for the groom's house.

In Puthan Street also, there was this same bustle and hurry. Women, children and the wedding *nadaswaram*—when all these combine, can anyone escape the noise?

The lamp was lit in the house—on the front platform. The men sat on the carpet. A broken pot was half-filled with husk, lit up, fanned into a flame by the goldsmith blowpipe, the gold held and turned over a flame with forceps and melted. Iyamperumal Achari was in charge of making the *mangalyam* (thali). The women made the *kolavai* noises to their hearts' content.

Then, there was the feast. The whole town was present. The party was rich, so the feast was also good. It was a heavy meal full of all the usual good things—plenty of vegetables, *aviyal*, potato *podimas*, *pachadi*, *kichidi*, mango *gose*, *pappadam*, dry-fried things, sugared banana chips, ghee, lentils, sambhar, *pulisseri*, rasam, three kinds of payasams, and lastly, buttermilk. It was indeed a feast.

After the meal when we were all ready to leave, Papathi Aunt stayed us saying, "Stay a little… I shall give some food. The food of the gold-thali-melting ceremony should be eaten by the bride also. I shall give you some for her." She brought the food and all the items in separate vessels for Nagu Akka. We carried it home.

Days sped by, one after another. We heard that some people had gone from the bridegroom's house to Tirunelveli and bought the silk the bride was to wear at the *muhurtam*[3]: blouse, inner petticoat, and even a dress for the bride's sister, Salam.

Father went to Nagercoil and bought all the necessary clothes. He was told that he too had to buy a silk sari for his daughter and so he did, in the colour of the brinjal flower. For Mother, he bought a long 14 cubit *kandangi*[4]. It was bright green in colour. Aachi too got a new unbleached sari. Unnamalai Akka got a silk sari in the colour of *kanakambaram* flowers[5]. For me, he bought an all-yellow dress, and an unbleached mulmul[6] dhoti. Salam got a silk petticoat all covered with flowers and a blouse to match. Above all this, Father bought for the son-in-law-to-be, white silk clothes, 8 cubits of lace-bordered silk dhoti, and a silk upper cloth with bright colours. It glittered with gold lace inwork.

In the meantime, the wedding invitations arrived printed on glossy, silky paper. They smelt sweet. For the guests from within the town, we gave the invitations personally. For those out of town, we sent the invitations via post.

Two days before the wedding, the courtyard was covered with the pandal and a silken canopy. The house acquired a majestic appearance—an air of prosperity.

In the middle of the courtyard was the wedding platform, looking quite distinguished. On four sides of it stood four small pillars, glittering with brightly-coloured paper and blue, green, and red tinsel. On top was a pot, shaped like a temple tower, and on top of that, a deep green parrot, ready to fly away at a moment's notice. It too was made of paper, but looked very real.

In the backyard of the house was the cooking area, in which new oven-pits had been dug.

Vembu Iyer, the cook, gave in a list of things that would be required for cooking.

"When you buy things for the wedding, you should make an auspicious start by first buying turmeric," instructed Aachi. Accordingly, turmeric was bought first and then the groceries, vegetables, fruits, long banana leaf bundles, pots of curds—the house was chockful of things.

"Papathi had asked for two thousand sweets. Shouldn't we give her atleast a thousand...five hundred *murukkus*[7], three hundred *alenge*[8], two hundred cakes—and the sweetened flour yet unmade." We had to prepare all this.

Spreading a mat and covering it with white cloth, the *murukkus* were twisted to dry on them before they were deep fried. Unnamalai Aachi was holding forth with pride to all the women helping her in the making of *murukkus*. I was delighted to see the way they twisted *murukkus*—whatskill, what beauty there was. On the fire was a large vessel of coconut oil. When the oil was sufficiently hot, without disturbing their twists, the *murukkus* were put into it and fried. The sizzling sound when each piece slid into the oil was a delight to hear. The aroma made my tongue water.

There were barely two days to the wedding. The sweet flour should precede the bride to the groom's house after the wedding. The girl should prepare the flour sent for her, "and then, we have to make two hundred cakes with this flour," said Ponamu Aachi.

"Run, you fellow, and tell the groom's mother that we are readying the sweetened flour and bid her come to see it. Run," bade Unnamalai Aachi.

I ran to the groom's house and took Papathi Aunt back with me. Meanwhile, the wooden mortar had been rolled into the centre of the verandah, and before it stood Nagu Akka, shy and frowing with the long wooden pestle in hand.

"Oh dear girl, Nagu. Your mother-in-law has arrived… O Papathi, take three pieces of turmeric and put it in the mortar. Let your daughter-in-law-to-be powder it." This was the head-shaking granny, all the while shaking her head. Everybody laughed with pure delight and happiness. Nagu Akka tried to hide her face behind the thin round pestle.

Papathi Aunt put the turmeric pieces in the mortar and when Mother said, "Start grinding." Nagu Akka wielded the wooden pestle with a will. And all the women standing around made the *kolavai* noises thrice running.

"Enough. Now if we add the prepared rice, the mix will be ready." Papathi took the soaked rice that was kept ready in the palm-leaf receptacle and put three handfuls of it into the mortar. The women made the *kolavai* noise and sang. Nagu Akka wielded the pestle with all the might of her weak arms. After a short while, Aunt Thayee said "She is only a young girl, let us not tax her too much," and gripping the pestle herself, set about grinding the flour with skill and strength.

In the inner verandah, tailor Thangaiyan, assisted by two boys, was stuffing two bright satin mattresses and four high pillows with silk cotton.

Everything was festive and busy.

All the relatives from out of town had begun to arrive.

On the eve of the wedding was the vegetable cutting ceremony. All the items were displayed on banana leaves and cut into pieces, after they were named.

Everyone was talking loudly, happily, joking with each other. It was quite heartening.

In the makeshift backyard kitchen, the smoke began to rise.

All the necessary garlands of flowers had been delivered. Rows of flowers were strung tastefully all over the pandal and on the wedding platform.

At the outer gate of the house, the stems of two big plantain trees cut at the lower ends and with two bright thrusting red banana flowers were tied, one on each side; the row of leaves, which adorned the rim of the roof was green and cool to the eye.

In the street before the house, under the pandal was spread white beach sand. It looked as if new prosperity had dawned on the house and family.

Under the street pandal, inside in the courtyard and verandahs were huge, hired carpets either spread or kept in readiness to be rolled out as and when necessary.

The night before the wedding, no one could sleep. There was so much to attend to... Father looked tired. He had been busy all the time. Every now and then, he would get angry, run about from place to place and shout at someone or other. Heaven knows how he got the money for all these things.

Eight

In school, the last bell rang.

Carrying his books, and full of anxiety about what was happening back in the house, Diravi was setting out swiftly towards home, when someone called him. He turned back to see who it was.

Sasi was running towards him. "Diravi, how many times am I to call you?" he asked in a curious mixture of Tamil and Malayalam.

"Yes, what is it?" Diravi asked, walking slowly. Sasi came along with him, his satchel full of books.

Sasi was of the same age as Diravi. He was as delicate as a girl, charming and very fair skinned. Dark hair crowned his head; it fell on his perspiring face, irritating him.

"It's nothing. Mother called you; she asked you to visit us at home," he replied.

"Whatever for?" Diravi was puzzled.

"I don't know. But Mother told me that after school, I was to take you home. Mother said it was something important."

Diravi wondered why Sasi's mother wanted to see him. Would it be to ask him about his Nagu Akka and her husband?

"When did your Mother ask you about me?" Diravi inquired.

"She has been telling me for the last two days. I forgot yesterday and the day before. Today, she insisted that I bring you home."

She had been searching for him for the past two days. Then it could not be about Nagu Akka. The reason must be something else.

"Let's go."

Both of them left the road and turned into a lane. On both sides of the lane, tall trees—jack, coconut, palm, and—mango cast their shade; the shade was not too dark in the setting sun. The four o'clock sunlight, yellow and wan—when it fell on one's body, was pleasant and not too warm.

From the top of the palm trees, men were talking across spaces to one another, carrying on their gossip from on high. A few got down with a characteristic scraping sound and were ascending other trees skilfully to finish their work before dark.

The boys crossed the dense garden and walked along the edge of the fields by the side of an irrigation canal in which the water murmured pleasantly.

Ordinarily, Diravi would have talked to Sasi enthusiastically. But now, he was silent, lost in thought, putting Sasi off his mood. He did not want to disturb Diravi either and walked along silently, watching the workers singing in the fields.

He thought of Nagu Akka and felt sorry. Now, in his mind, her place was taken by Ammukkutti Ammachi—Sasi's mother's mother. How did it happen? Diravi wondered.

Why could she have sent for him now?

Diravi was very fond of Ammukkutti Ammachi. She talked to him lovingly, calling him "child", only as his own granny did. She would look out for things to give him whenever he went to her house.

Ammachi's son, Sasi's father, used to call his wife (Sasi's mother) Thangi. She too was fond of Diravi and would make much of him whenever he visited her. Amminikutti, her daughter, would also be extremely affectionate to Diravi. She was only a year or two older than Salam, his sister.

Why were all the members of that house affectionate towards him?

It was possibly because he was a grand-nephew of Koonangai Paatta, Diravi explained to himself.

He was dimly aware that Sasi was asking him something.

"What is it Sasi? What did you ask?"

"Aren't you well?"

"No, no! I'm fine."

"I don't see your usual enthusiasm and spirit."

"Oh! Nothing like that." But Diravi was silent again, lost in his own thoughts.

Sasi also did not talk after that. Both of them went along silently.

Sasi's house stood in the midst of a coconut grove just ahead.

Sasi crossed into the grove and announced loudly and happily, "Amma, Amma, Diravi has come! Diravi has come!"

From the simple coconut-frond-covered hut came Ammukkutti Ammachi. She wore no blouse, but had tied her *mundu*[1] right upto her neck; the *mundu* had a broad black border. Her hair was completely white. Her forehead was adorned with sacred ash. She wore no earrings, but the holes in her ear lobes proclaimed that she had worn them for long. Her teeth showed the red of habitual betel leaf chewers.

"Come, come… I sent for you. I told him to bring you today after school. Diravi comes rarely these days…" She too spoke in a strange mixture of Tamil and Malayalam.

The hut had only a mud floor, but it was neat, decorative, soft, and clean, with frequent applications of cowdung. The walls were also made of mud, and cool. Wooden shelves, carved tastefully, stood along the walls. A small, simple, but beautiful, house.

On the outer verandah were placed two wooden benches together. At one end lay a pillow rolled up in a mat. Perhaps Sasi's father slept on that bench. There was a small table beside it. Sasi's books lay on it, but there was no disorder there. A hurricane lantern with a smoke-encrusted chimney hung from the roof, oscillating in the breeze. At night, it would be set on Sasi's table for him to read by.

"Sit down child; it has been many days since I last saw you." Ammachi took him by the hand, led him to the bench, and made him sit on it.

"Oh, is it Diravi? Have you forgotten all of us?" asked Sasi's mother, Thangammai, emerging from the hut, pushing the long corner of her *mundu* into the upper part of her jacket. Evidently, she had been busy in the kitchen.

She was about 30 or 35 years old, came from Thiruvattaru and was still beautiful.

From behind her, the bright face of Amminikkutti was visible, peering out.

"Diravi Etten[2]," she said.

The was something in that child's face which attracted him; her eyes were lively. She was a charming child.

"It is Diravi Etten…it is!" she shouted with glee.

"Eh, daughter, go and get him something to drink!" ordered Ammachi to her daughter-in-law.

"I shall bring it," said Thangammai and went in.

Ammachi sat on the floor near the bench. She drew the betel pestle and mortar from beneath the bench and leisurely prepared her betel leaves and nuts.

Coconut trees grew all round the place. In the distance, the fields were green and the farmers working in the fields sang with gusto. They were watering the fields. Above it all, a cloudless blue sky.

It was a quiet, peaceful abode.

Suddenly, memories of his sister crowded in on him; he had managed to forget her for a while. He felt extremely sad.

Ammachi did not notice it. Evidently, nothing about what was happening in his house had reached these people. When Sasi's father returned from Nagercoil at 9 in the night, he might bring them the news. He was a clerk to a lawyer in Nagercoil.

"Child, I have been expecting you for the past few days."

Slowly, Ammachi began to talk of what she wanted of

him. "You should ask your Paatta to come here and see us when he can, as soon as he can."

Diravi thought he saw her eyes filling with tears.

"I shall tell him to come immediately, Ammachi. I shall tell him as soon as I get home."

At this moment, Thangammai brought roasted palm-root spliced and coconut shavings mixed together and a tumbler full of hot palm-sugar coffee and placed them before Diravi.

"Why all this?" Diravi asked.

"Eat it child. We are also related to you."

Amminikkutti could not contain her laughter and happiness.

Ammachi had accumulated enough betel juice in her mouth to make it impossible for her to talk. She sat where she was, turned her face outwards, and spat forcefully with practised skill.

"Child, tell him privately. Don't tell him as you once did in the presence of Ponamu and Ananji; they will begin to quarrel…" she warned him, laughing. Thangammai too laughed with her mother-in-law.

Diravi was embarrassed at seeing both women laughing—as if it were at him. "I shall be careful. I will tell him privately. I remember what happened that time." Yes, he knew what the matter was. After the quarrel, he had talked at length with Unnamalai Aachi and learnt the whole story about Ammachi and Koonangani Paatta.

When Diravi took leave of them and set out, Amminikkutti was standing there watching him with wide, unblinking eyes.

Nine

Daylight was fading into dusk. There was no one else on the pathway. Diravi was walking along slowly, thinking about Ammachi and all he had come to know about her.

Like him, Sasi too had been in the same school right from the beginning. But Diravi had come to know of him only the year before. Sasi often called him to his house.

Ammachi was overjoyed to see Diravi in her house.

"Oh my golden boy…" she exclaimed smelling him over the head. She held him in a close embrace and kissed him, wafting a smell of stale betel leaves into his face.

Often, Sasi persuaded Diravi to go home with him. There he was an honoured guest. More than the sweets and other eatables they gave him, it was their obvious affection for him that drew him. Ammachi, Sasi's father, mother, all of them treated him with love and affection.

One day, Ammachi asked him, "Child, I want you to do something for me…Can you? Diravi had agreed.

Ammachi whispered in his ears, "Your Paatta—he who lives in the house opposite yours, your granny's brother… Will you tell him that I want to see him? It has been a long time since I saw him."

When Diravi returned home, the old man, his Paatta, was in the inner verandah pounding betel nuts. Near him sat his wives Ponamu Aachi and Ananji Aachi talking about something which Diravi could not understand.

"Paatta, Ammukkutti Aachi told me to ask you to visit her because she has not seen you for a long time. You go and see her." No sooner had Diravi said it than Paatta's wives began berating him roundly and loudly. Diravi's words were the signal for the start of a wordy warfare... Ponamu Aachi and Ananji Pillai Aachi called Paatta all sorts of names. Ammukkutti Ammachi also came in for a lot of abuse.

"Ammu's games are not yet over. That poisonous woman is old, but sends for her lover even now...abominable whore...hopeless prostitute."

The two women called Ammukkutti Ammachi all sorts of names. Paatta's sons, Malu Pillai Uncle, Picha Pillai Uncle, and Andi Pillai Uncle, all three had gone to Ammachi's house and abused her roundly.

Paatta flushed with embarrassment. He looked helplessly at Diravi. Diravi did not understand what the trouble was. It was all very confusing.

However much he thought about it, he could not understand why. So, after the hullabaloo had ceased somewhat, he submitted the problem to his last court of appeal, Unnamalai Aachi.

"What is this Aachi? Sasi and I are great friends at school. When he called me home, I went along. His granny treats me with genuine affection and love. She wanted to meet Paatta—I told him that…and you saw how my two grannies abused Paatta and Ammachi. It seemed that they would never cease. All the listeners made fun of me…for what I don't know. Even Mother and Father called me an ass. Why all this hhubbub? I am unable to understand."

Evidently, Aachi had come to understand what the matter was. "Ah ha, so that is the matter, is it? So that is why his two wives tore him to pieces. What is that fellow's name…Pasi."

"Not Pasi, but Sasi. His full name Sasidharan Nair."

"Then, he must be that Krishnan Kutty's son. Is he in your class?"

"Yes… but he is in the Malayalam section I am in the Tamil class. Who is that Krishnan Kutty?"

"He is also an uncle of yours," said Aachi and laughed loudly.

"How can he be an uncle of mine? He is a Nair, a Malayali. How can he?

"Like Picha Pillai, like Malu Pillai, and like Andi Pillai, Krishnan Kutty is also one of your uncles." She thought this was a great joke and continued laughing.

"Tell me plainly… How is he my uncle?"

Aachi looked around to check if anybody else was listening. Mother was busy in the kitchen, cooking utensils were being moved about noisily. Visalam, who had been reading in the light of the pedestal lamp, was sleeping, using the book as a pillow, the house was full of darkening shadows. This was Aachi's hour of rest; she and Diravi were alone on the front inner verandah. She had seen a bunch of coconut fronds going brown in the backyard, had dragged it in and was engaged in separating the leaves, removing the greener part, so that the stalks could be strung into a broom when there was a sufficient quantity of them. This was work which she loved to do. She had stretched her legs and was paring the prospective broomsticks with a penknife. It was an art that she had cultivated over many years; not a stick broke in her hands. This was the time when she was usually at her most expansive and expressive moods. She would talk to Diravi at these times as if he were grown up, without any condescension in her voice. She loved to tell him things which were sometimes beyond his understanding. Sometimes, she would glance round surreptitiously, and then tell him of her irritation with his mother; not that she had many such complaints.

Lowering her voice impressively, Aachi said, "Krishnan Kutty's mother is that Sasi's granny. Her name is Ammukkutti. Like Ponamu Aachi, like Ananji Pillai Aachi, she is also an Aachi to you." Aachi smiled meaningfully at Diravi and, as if letting him into a secret, she made eyes at him mischievously.

Diravi thought he understood. But he wanted to hear the whole thing from Aachi's mouth. He knew that at these expansive moments, she would tell him the complete story, because she enjoyed telling him what she knew.

"Then Ammukutti Ammachi is Koonangani Paatta's..." he stopped suggestively.

"She was your Paatta's keep."

Diravi was nonplussed for a moment at this assertion. He kept silent, looking up at Aachi.

"Oh child. In Tiruvancode, if you took the name of my father, Mootha Pillai[1] Mookandi Chettiar, a weeping child would close its mouth in fear. If any wedding or funeral took place in the town, a double portion was due to our house... that is what it meant to the eldest of the clan. He had a tuft of hair behind his head. He was tall and quite fair—a great personality. Also, he would wear his dhoti so, that swept the floor as he walked—so low would he wear it as a sign of his exalted state. When he spoke, all those who heard him shook in fear and respect. Even members of his immediate family would scurry about like rats. If he were in the house, I would invariably hide behind mother..."

"Was Koonangani Paatta not afraid of your father?"

"He was also afraid. But he was a darling son, born late, after much penance. As soon as he was born, they took him to the Sastha temple to acknowledge that he was God's gift to them."

"All the boys born to my mother before him died very young. They were afraid that he too might die early and were unduly fond of him. To prevent an early end, they made him wear a nose ring till he was ten. Father was much too fond of his only son. I was born ten years after him. There was a boy born between us, but he died when he was two, I was told..."

Stopping her story at this point, Aachi bade him bring the stone and mortar for her betel nuts. "I need it. Let me chew once." Preparing the betel nut in due fashion, she continued, "Wherever Father went, Koonangani Anna[2] would also accompany him."

She was lost in contemplation of those glorious times and could never cease talking of the bygone days and their greatness. Diravi had heard tales of these past splendours many times. He listened impatiently, waiting and hoping that she would eventually arrive at the story of his Paatta and Ammukkutti Ammachi.

"In those days, Father was the proprietor of many houses and fields and farms. The coconut gardens were big and the trees in them, numberless. If one began to pluck the coconuts from the north, before one arrived at the south boundary, the trees in the north would have borne coconuts again. The trees were of such quality that they yielded throughout the year and not only during what was called 'the season'. There were fields he owned in Muttam, Kurunthankode, Kumarakovil and other places. Old farms that were priceless…all of it has now vanished."

Aachi sighed as was her wont when she came to this part of the story. It was a sorrowful truth that when the wealthy past had to be compared with the bitter present, there was nothing else to do but sigh.

"Here, at Eraniyal too, there were land and fields and coconut gardens. The garden, in which Ammukkutti lives today, also belonged to Father in those days, mango, jackfruit, tamarind and pinnai trees, coconut-palms…and endless variety of trees. In the house he was a valuer of precious gems and gold. At any time of the day, men would call on him for his expert opinion. He was torn between the two. He could not attend to his fields as well as the gem trade. So, he gave his lands on contract to various dependable persons. Even then, every day in the morning, he would make time to visit his contractors and tenants and collect his dues. He kept a good carriage for that. It was a well-made cart with a spring axle… Koonangani was your age at the time. As soon as the cart came, he would run to it and get in, next to the driver. Father would not object; he would take him along. Coming back, the cart would be loaded with tender bunches of palms, or honey, jackfruit, or mangoes of the Tiryvarangan variety, or if any of these things was not in season, home-made palm sugar jiggery just out of the pan."

The old woman was rambling along and not coming to the point. Diravi was impatient. "Oh Aachi, it was about Ammachi and Paatta I wanted to hear. You are babbling of other things…" Then, putting the betel nut into her mouth, Aachi laid aside the pestle and mortar and went back to making the broom. She disliked being hurried through her storytelling, especially when she herself was enjoying the telling.

"You hasty duckling… He who waits enough to cook should wait to let what is cooked to cool down. I am coming to that, but where did I stop? If you talk of one thing, I forget the other…"

She could not recall and Diravi had to remind her. Then she continued:

"Koonangani Anna was the favourite, the only son; he was his father's darling.

In those days, there were not so many schools as there are now. He did not take well to studies. As soon as he could stumble through the alphabet, he left school; he thought he had learnt too much. To teach me my alphabet and arithmetic, Father engaged a lady teacher, who came everyday. Wait, I shall recollect her name... Yes, she was called Eli. She was a Nadar woman. She had become a Christian. I still remember her very well. She wore a brooch at the shoulder, gathering a sari to a point. She parted her hair to the right, and was clean and pleasant. She was charming. I was seven or eight years old at that time; Brother Koonangani was 18 or thereabouts. As soon as she came, he would begin to dance attendance on her; to grin, to talk to her on some excuse, to give her things, to show her this or that—any excuse would serve."

The way the old woman said these things clearly indicated to Diravi that this was not exemplary behaviour on the part of his Paatta.

"A thief of long standing will one day be found out, says the proverb. One day Father came to know of all this. You should have seen his anger when he learnt of his son's behaviour. There was a tamarind tree just to the opposite our house. He had Koonangani Anna tied to the tamarind tree and, selecting a supple branch, he mercilessly beat the life out of him. Brother squirmed like a worm with the pain and shame of it. No one could go near him and talk to Father or stop him. Mother was not like the modern wives. She was terribly afraid of her husband. Neighbours and our farm and field workers looked on, not knowing what to do. But Mother could not keep quiet; she had borne Anna. She wept aloud and threw her arms round her husband preventing him from beating the boy any more. My studies came to an end then and there. My lady teacher ceased to visit."

Ten

Diravi was walking along the lonely path, thinking of all that his Aachi had told him. "Ho Chettiar…going far?" asked a disembodied voice quite near. It was Anabaiyan, whose head alone was visible over the leaves of the trees.

"Not far. Just for a walk," said Diravi trying to laugh it off. But Anbaiyan laughed loud and long. "You are returning from Ammachi's house, aren't you?" he asked and laughed loudly again.

Diravi walked on, saying nothing in reply. He was immersed in thought, thinking of the story Aachi had told him and talking to himself. "Where did I stop…" I wanted to hear about Ammachi and Paatta, but Aachi was telling me at length about her teacher and the beating her brother took at the hands of her father. I got angry, I asked what the relation between Ammachi and Koonangani Paatta was and she told me all sorts of things which had no bearing on it.

Aachi could not contain her laughter at my anger. "Oh little one. What a temper you have. Why are you so eager to hear that Ammukkutti's story? Wait, I shall tell you. But that is not the only thing that occupies my mind—I have too many things to talk of. If I were young like you, my mind would be free of many memories, which filled my mind like an overcrowded dungheap. I have to rack my brains to remember what you ask…"

Aachi spat the betel juice and continued from where she had stopped.

"I didn't say all this about my teacher for nothing. Koonangani Anna's character became evident from then on. Only when you grant that, will you be able to understand what happened later. The teacher was the first; it led gradually to Ammukkutti… You can tell a man by what he is when young; his habits will continue till he dies."

"Whenever Father went to the fields, Brother also accompanied him. After the incident with the teacher, Father was sure that if the boy was allowed to continue without work, he would fall into bad ways very quickly. So, he gave him work. Father began to stay at home, attending to his business with the gems. All the other work devolved upon Koonangani Anna's youthful shoulders. Gathering the harvest, talking to the tenants, collecting and bringing home the coconuts, mangoes, jackfruits, and other produce from the gardens and fields—all this work became Brother's sole responsibility. He lived in the bullock cart with the spring axle. There was a cart driver called Velu, but Koonangani Anna was an expert himself. He would twist the tail of the bullock and cry 'drio' and get quite an amazing speed from the cart…"

I was alert. If allowed to go on about the driving of the cart, Aachi would never come to a stop. She would have begun telling me how many kinds of carts her Father had, the relative merits of each, the points about the bulls they'd had. Once she started on that, she would never arrive at Ammachi's story. But she continued, "Brother's expenses were mounting alarmingly. His accounting was short; he could not account for all the monies he received from the tenants. He would quarrel with Mother and occasionally take money from her also..."

"One Friday, Mother and I set out for Velli Malai[1] temple," Aachi said. "Father did not come. Velu drove the cart...You know Vellai Malai... Have you been there?" Aachi asked, leaving the story halfway. Aachi's asking me the question like that angered me. For a long time, she had been promising to take me to Velli Malai, but had not done so yet. I had not been there even once. I said in sorrow and in anger, "You've been promising to take me, but you haven't done it so far. How many times have you promised me?

Aachi laughed. "Child, next festive Friday, I shall certainly take you. It is uphill. Even if we go by the shortcut by way of Kurunthankode and Talaikkolam, it is at least three or three-and-a-half miles. Will you be able to walk the distance?"

I waxed angrier still. "Can't I walk? Only three miles... Didn't I walk with you to Mondakkadu. How many miles was that? Not only to Mondakkadu, but also to Kumarakovil. Didn't we walk? Did we go by car?" and she had pacified me.

"All right. We shall go on the last Friday of the next month. Just wait."

Even as he was walking along, thinking of the talk with Aachi, Diravi felt sad that he had never been to Velli Malai. So many last Fridays of months had come and gone, but Aachi had not kept her promise. Many of his friends had been and had returned full of stories about Velli Malai. When a party of his friends set out next, he would also go and not wait for Aachi.

Aachi said, "One should see Velli Malai on the last Friday of a month. Pilgrims come from far off places. It is festive and very crowded. Gruel is stored in big stone troughs and served to all who come—with ash pumpkin curry, it is delicious. It is like God's amrit[2]."

Aachi had clicked her tongue to show how tasty it was. She had been expansive about the virtues of the gruel served free by the temple.

"We were going round the temple, doing the necessary prostration and worship, Mother and I, when two Malayali ladies calling out 'Amme, Amme' approached us. One was about 40 years old; the other just 15 or 16..."

I pricked up my ears, all agog to hear what would come next. Aachi had continued, "That was Ammukkutti and her mother. My eyes were dazzled by Ammukutti's beauty. What a pity that she was so charming! She had colour that baffled description; her face was beauty itself. Her hair was long and glossy and tied up in a bun. She was wearing a tamarind-leaf-border mundu, and a lace choli. She herself shone like the lace in her cloth… I am charmed to think of her even now, after all this time."

Aachi was lost in the contemplation of that past moment of a vision of beauty. If Aachi was affected this way, what could poor Koonangani Paatta have done? Could one blame him?

"Look at our Chetti women... When they wear silk, they do so inelegantly without any style at all, winding it round and round as you would on a cheap doll. But the Malayali girls bathe, adorn, and dress themselves well and seeing them is like seeing goddesses in person. When I see a Malayali girl in the temple, I wonder whether to prostrate before the girl or the goddess. Mother knew who it was. She was the daughter of the tenant of the coconut grove and garden, here at Eraniyal. She was Ammu's mother, Bhavani. Bhavani and her daughters had come to our house, when the girl was much younger."

"We talked to them for a little while, had a darshan[3] of the lights, and going back in the cast, the driver Velu told us the story in bits, stammering in fear: 'I have eaten your salt and I should not wish you harm. If I do you harm, what little I eat will sour in my stomach.' With such introductions he told us what he wanted to say. Koonangani Anna was friendly with Ammu—a long standing affair... Brother always stayed with them at Eraniyal. 'He would suddenly set off for the garden. At first, I thought it was about the produce. At long last, I learnt the truth. When he realised that I knew, he told me it was essential for Father not to find out. I tried to plead with him, but he would not listen.' Velu lowered his voice and added, 'Please don't tell anyone that I told you the story.

Let not the young master know. He is young. It is natural for him to be like this. It is not uncommon in the world. Try to talk to him in private and correct him. It is no use blaming him; at this age, he should be married and living with a wife; then everything would be all right.'"

Aachi finished readying the broom she had been making. "Mother warned me that I should not talk to anyone about it, much less to Father. If Father had found out he could have murdered the boy. She could not consult anyone about it, but she could not contain herself either. She was sorely tired."

"But in course of time everyone became aware of it. At long last, even Father found out. But by that time, Ammachi had become the mother of a boy, Krishnan Kutty, father of Sasi, and not even my Father could do anything about it. But Koonangani Anna stood firm; he refused to leave Ammukkutti. He was a grown man; he could not be beaten like a boy; he was so firm and obstinate about, it that nothing could solve the problem. Father was ashamed of his son's behaviour and, at last, died of shame."

Eleven

Walking back alone, the way seemed long to Diravi. With Sasi around, the way had not seemed so long. But he did not feel tired of what his Aachi had told him about it all. Diravi's mind suddenly flashed to his sister's sorrowful face in his mind's eye. "Why had Brotheer-in-law cast Nagu Akka away?" was the question that occupied his mind.

A red bus from Nagercoil and overcrowded to the full passed on. Diravi crossed the road. At East Street, passing the Singa Vinayaka temple, Diravi raised both hands, bringing them together before his face in obeisance.

The street was crowded at that time. Unnamalai Aachi was standing in front of the house, worried that her grandson was late. When he came near enough to hear, she said, "Eh, boy; where did you go after school. Even at noon, you did not eat...."

Diravi entered the house, saying "Sasi took me to his house."

Father was not at home. Nagu Akka still lay face down on the platform. Some women from the neighbourhood had gathered round, trying to console her in a babble of voices.

Salam was playing with some friends in the courtyard.

Aachi went as far as the courtyard and said loudly, "Eh Kuttiamme, give the boy his food... He is hungry."

Diravi went into the kitchen and sat down to eat. He looked up at his mother, as she asked him where he had been so long after school. Her face was dark with endured sorrow. She was not her usual self. He told her the tale of how he went to Ammachi's house in the garden. "Where is Father?" he asked.

"He went to see the town's trustees. They are going to discuss your sister's case, you know?" Diravi too was stricken with sorrow seeing the agony in her tone and manner.

Aachi was engaged in sweeping and cleaning the front of the house. As soon as she swept it, Mother washed it with water. Mother washed her face and marked her forehead afresh and looked a little better than she had some time ago. She looked at her daughter, and said, "Eh Nagammai... How long will you keep sobbing like this? Don't be stupidly obstinate. If you lie on an empty stomach like this, you will be more upset. Father has gone out to see what your fate is to be. leave it all to God and attend to the ordinary business of the day. Come on, it is dusk. Go, wash your face, and at least, take some palm-jaggery water... don't lie prone like this at dusk."

Half-heartedly Nagu Akka rose and went to the well. Aachi too had washed up, taken sacred ash from the vessel hanging from the rafters of the inner verandah and applied it to her forehead saying, "Oh Lord, Velayudha, my God."

Diravi was impatient at the thought of staying home, doing nothing. He felt burdened within, weak and restless. He didn't feel like reading either. Where could he go?

Suddenly, he remembered Ammachi's message to Koonangani Paatta. Let me go and see if he is at home.

It was dark in the street illuminated only in patches by light from the lamps lit inside the contiguous houses. It did not dispel the darkness, but made the shadows darker. Those in the street and those sitting on the front platforms, talking, looked at Diravi with pity and commiseration, or so he thought; though he knew that the feeling itself was illusory. He crossed the street to reach Koonangani Paatta's house and went up the steps into it. The outer door was closed, but it opened when he pushed it. He couldn't see anyone inside. On the fore platform, a single light burned, shedding a faint light. From the kitchen came rays of light that dimly penetrated the outer hall. To the left was a small room, from which he thought he could hear two persons whispering. He peeped into the room and was surprised by what he saw. Aunt Nilappillai's son, Chidambaram, was dozing, book in hand. Chidambaram's teacher Kumaraswamy, otherwise known as Korami, was sitting in a chair close to him, almost on his, was Nilappillai Aunt. A sooty hurricane light was their only witness.

When he took in the scene, Diravi started perspiring all over. He withdrew from the doorway and tried to hide. What a shameless hussy she was, a widow… She…

He stood still for a little while and grew alert again at the loud laughter of two persons from within the room.

"Teh, Teh."

What shameless persons these are—he is a primary school teacher, this Korami...lost his wife only six or seven months ago...comes here on the excuse of giving private lessons to Chidambaram. What a hopeless fellow he is. What has happened to the mother, Ponamu Aachi, of this Nilappillai Aunt. Ananji Pillai Aachi too usually goes round the house prying into nooks and corners. What has happened to her now? What happened to the uncles and Koonangani Paatta himself?

Diravi wanted to leave without making a noise, or being noticed by anyone. But as he was leaving, Ponamu Aachi looked out of the kitchen and saw him: "Who is it? Diravi? Eh, boy, come. Come in here. Why do ou stand there like a guest waiting for an invitation?"

Unable to avoid going in, he entered. She was minding the oven. "This oven refuses to ignite. Korami Teacher is struggling with Chidambaram's lessons; the fellow refuses to learn. I thought I would prepare a glass of coffee with palm-jaggery water for Korami, but the oven refuses to cooperate." The oven was smoking, and so was she, in frustration.

Diravi sat on the kitchen doorstep. That was his usual place whenever he came to their house. He was wondering whether it was Chidambaram or Chidambaram's mother, who was Korami Teacher's pupil. He almost blurted it out, but restrained himself with difficulty, and instead asked, "How old is Chidambaram?"

"He is all of five years. This year, he had to be put to school. It has been four years since he lost his father…that scoundrel died comfortably when the boy was a year old, leaving her a widow without means."

The old woman would call the late Hariharaputra Pillai all sorts of names at least nine times in a day; unless she did so, she could not sleep. He had married Nilappillai Aunt three years before he fell ill with smallpox. She was afraid that she and her one-year-old son might get infected. Ponamu Aachi was sent for and as soon as she arrived, she quarrelled with her daughter's father-in-law and petulantly asked, "Did I give my daughter in marriage to your son so that she could catch the smallpox from him and die? You attend to him; I shall take my daughter and grandson with me." She brought them from Midalam to Eraniyal. Even when he died, she had not sent her daughter or anybody else for the last rites. Koonangani Paatta tried to persuade someone to go, but no one heeded him. He had then gone on his own.

Diravi bore a memory of Nilappillai Aunt that he could never lie down. Some eight years ago, when he was a small boy, his mother had sent him with some kolam powder to be given to this aunt. Dressed in a red sari, Aunt was sitting with her mouth all red with betel chewing. While giving her the coloured powder, his fingers had touched her inadvertently. "Eh?" She flipped off the dhoti he had been wearing. He was angry and ashamed and had returned to his mother, weeping. Everybody made fun of him for having touched a woman during her monthly period thus becoming polluted;

he had to rinse and dry his dhoti. To be stripped by a woman and to run away weeping—the memory smarted whenever Nilappillai Aunt or Ponamu Aachi reminded him of it.

"But where is Paatta or Ananji Pillai Aachi, or the uncles…are all of them away?" Diravi asked.

"Uncle went to the Vinayaka temple… The elder sister has gone down to gossip with our neighbours. Your uncle will be sorry if anyone said anything against her, you know. Her son, Andi Pillai, will be playing cards somewhere. He is a rich fellow—what else has he to do? Picha Pillai and Iyah have gone to the bazaar."

Meanwhile, the palm-jaggery water, otherwise called coffee, was ready. She gave him a tumbler-full of it and filled another tumbler and said, "Let us go and give it to Korami teacher."

Diravi laughed to himself. At what stage of their romance would they be now? He walked behind Ponamu Aachi. Chidambaram was awake but sleepy and Korami Teacher was teaching him his ABC. There was no sign of Nilappillai Aunt anywhere there. Had he really seen her there? Diravi wondered.

He spent some time talking with Ponamu Aachi about the gossip of the town. But there was no sign of Paatta's early return. Thinking he could see him later, Diravi took leave of Ponamu Aachi and stepped out of the house, only to see his Paatta coming along the street, adorned with all the signs of a visit to the temple—his forehead, chest, and even ears bore signs of the sacred ash. Diravi approached and whispered to him that Ammachi wished to see him. And then he went home.

Twelve

The clock on community president Velu Pillai's house struck 10. Diravi, who was sitting near his father, was terribly sleepy. He thought of going home, but wanted to know Nagu Akka's fate. Even if he went home, his heart would linger behind.

Just two houses from the temple of Pillayar, on the left side of the street stretching east to west, was Velu Pillai's tiled and terraced house.

On the big platform running along the front of the house, from a beam on the roof hung a big lantern shedding its light, and surrounded by insects. Diravi watched them, fascinated. His mind began to wander. All the trustees were there, except Puthan Street Vinyaka Peruman Pillai They had sent someone to call him. A few of them were laughing amongst themselves, they were not at all sorry about Nagu Akka's plight.

What had happened to Brother-in-law? He did not look my way even once but sat in his corner of the mat, distance and aloof. There were a few men around him, evidently supporting him.

In support of my Father, were myself and Koonangani Paatta… Who else? Our neighbour Annamalai Pillai. I am a small boy and could only look on. What did I know of the law to talk to them about it? Finally, Vinayaka Perumal Pillai arrived. What a belly! All the important people of the town were there; it was crowded.

Papathi Aunt's youngest brother, Odayan Pillai, along with her sister's son-in-law, Thanu Pillai, and Puthan Street-Ekkimatan Pillai took turns to set out their case in loud voices. Though the words rang clear, I could not understand what they were saying. I wondered whether the others understood it either.

Paatta spoke clearly and very much to the point. "This is wrong. They have married a girl and are seeking to spoil her whole life six months later. How can a woman live without her husband? What will happen to her? This is a crime against womanhood, which they have to expiate and suffer for. It is a grievous sin. This is an action that will bring shame to the whole town…", but no one was listening to him.

Velu Pillai whispered in the ears of Brother-in-law. But he was adamant. "Whatever others might say, I won't allow that girl near me in this life! She…she…she..." He acted as if he had a great secret to reveal about her, but only hummed and hawed. Father was aghast and weighed down. Our neighbour, Annamalai Pillai, was angry. "Nonsense! What kind of humiliation is this? Why make a secret of it all? The secrets of the palace reach the market-place. Tell us what is wrong with the girl…" he challenged Brother-in-law loudly.

"I didn't want to disclose the secret so oopenly...because I sympathize with her. I wonder what I should say. Well, even though she looks like a woman, she… she…" Brother-in-law was overcome with emotion and could not proceed further, rolling his eyes wildly. Had he no brains? Who could doubt that Nagu Akka was all woman? Brother-in-law continued with, "Why talk at all? Send for a doctor and have her examined. Why should I say more? But I shall have to say this. It was wrong of them to have palmed her off as a woman and arranged her marriage. It was sin."

Brother-in-law would not define what the matter was, but went on for a long time like this. Two or three of the townsfolk spoke on our behalf. Hearing this, Brother-in-law's supporters made a lot of noise trying to shout them down.

Diravi fought hard to keep awake. His eyelids were heavy and would not stay open. He was surprised that they were still in the trustee's house; the talk was not yet over. He heard Annamalai Pillai's voice, "You can control an elephant but can you control men said to be endowed with minds? If they decide that the girl is not for them, then they will have to return all the dowry and gifts they received at the time of the wedding. That is only right."

Papathi was ready with her reply. "It is not right or fitting that we should talk in this manner. We have fed her big belly for all of these six months. Who is to compensate us for that? We too gave her jewels, clothes, vessels, etc… Who will pay us for that?"

She was a miser, the worst of misers…else would she have talked like this? Diravi thought he heard his father shouting in reply, but he did not fully comprehend what was said. His limbs ached. How long could he sit up like this. There was no space to stretch his limbs. Someone was talking loudly. "We should come to some decision. Say it once and for all."

Ekkimatan Pillai on Brother-in-law's side was emphatic and louder. He shouted, "What more is there to say and how shall we say it with greater finality?" he asked.

"If that is so, you should return the dowry items and the money received. You have spoilt the girl and her life. You will bear the burden of that sin. Mookan can find another wife. What wil be the fate of this poor girl? She will have to live without a husband for the rest of her life."

Someone made a fatalistic remark, "She was fated to live like that. What can we do? The sins of a past life…"

Diravi must have nodded off to sleep again, because he woke up to hear Brother-in-law or someone else saying loudly, "How many times are we tell you! It is like talking to the deaf! The land you gave her is in her name. Like a used leaf, we have thrown her out. We don't need the girl any longer."

It was all quite confusing as far as Diravi was concerned.

Thirteen

The house was in mourning. No one talked with anyone else. Each felt that he or she had committed a crime. They even avoided looking at each other.

Nagu Akka lay on her stomach most of the time, weeping either in the dark inner room or in the passage. These days, Mother was always angry with Salam. One never knew when Father came in for a meal and went out to mind the fields. When chewing betel or in the middle of some talk, Father would pause absentmindedly, lost in his own thoughts. Aachi would say, "What a despicable fellow! This sin will follow him and punish him," and would go in and try to console Nagu Akka.

The only person unaffected to any appreciable extent was Salam. She went to school, and played with her friends as usual. But Diravi was bitter. He did not remember how he returned home with his Father that night or how he went to sleep. Even the town trustees had failed to bring his sister and Brother-in-law together. What would happen to her now?

His mind was active and he suffered. A great burden bore him down, at school and at home. For five or six days, no one asked him to read his books. Every one of his schoolmates looked askance at him; they knew what had happened. In the streets, those who met him asked him about what had happened. Most were concerned, some just curious.

It was a holiday. They were playing a game with sticks among the trees. Diravi had won the game, but his friend, Ambalavanan, would not concede that he was right. Madevan sided with Ambalavanan. Others like Kuttalam, the oldest among the boys playing, kept aloof from the developing quarrel. Diravi, angry, said one thing, the other side said another—words not found in any dictionary flew about. Then, the other side said, "Everybody knows about your sister. Sevantha Perumal Pillai threw her out because, because…"

Diravi did not want to wait to hear the end of the sentence. But before he could say or do anything, Kuttalam leapt at them and beat them till their noses bled. "I am dead!" cried Ambalavanan as he fell. Then he got up and ran away with his friends without turning back. Only after they had fled the field did Kuttalam approach Diraviam and console him, "Merely saying the word 'fire' will not start the blaze. Someone must have instructed them to say these things. Pay no attention to these fools. They are numbskulls and idiots." He stroked Diravi's back soothingly. Diravi was impressed by Kuttalam and was beginning to like him. If Kuttalam had not been present, those fellows would have said something worse and shamed him further. It was a mistake on his part to have expected to forget his worries by playing with them. Usually boys from good homes did not play with Kuttalam, because he was socially their inferior and unfit to be with boys like

Diravi. But now, he had come to Diravi's help. "The dogs bark at the sun. Does the sun mind? Let us not worry about them. Mookan, your brother-in-law is to blame for all this; it is he who should be dealt with," said Kuttalam further. How right he was. Diravi looked up to him with new confidence.

Kuttalam also lived in Puthan Street. His father Thirukootan Pillai was considered a simpleton. His mother Pichamuthu had died some four years ago. He was not a good student and was repeating the 8th class. His grandmother forced him to go to school. "If I don't pass this year also, I shall work at weighing and measuring things in some shop," he used to say. What else could he do? How long would his father continue to support him? He had no job. It was Kuttalam's grandmother who did some household work and, with great difficulty, earned something to feed them. How long could she continue?

Kuttalam was not rich, but he was healthy. No one thought well of him. He did not listen to his father. Some evenings he went home. On others, he did not. He did not behave respectfully towards his elders or the trustees. He talked disrespectfully of those persons he knew had done wrong. He used to make fun of the servile, telling them, "Make obeisance, your master goes." His speech was sharp; his arms were long. No one had a good word for him, but no one interfered with him either.

After that day's incident, Diravi began to seek out Kuttalam. Only with him could he talk frankly and freely. It comforted him to talk to Kuttalam.

One day, coming back after school, Kuttalam leapt up on a hired bicycle and told Diravi, "I shall teach you also to cycle."

Sasi, who was walking with Diravi, whispered something in his ears. Diravi was surprised and asked him, "Really. Did he come yesterday?"

"When I went back from school I saw Grandfather in my house. I was told that he had come at noon..."

Koonangani Paatta came to your house at noon and when did he return?"

"In the evening, at seven or so."

Diravi remembered the message he had delivered on behalf of Ammachi secretly to his Paatta.

Don't you want to know why Granny wanted to meet Grandfather?" Sasi asked tartly.

"Do you know?" Diravi asked, his interest aroused, "It is a great secret, but I know. Diravi should not repeat it to anyone," said Sasi. "You know my father's sister, Bhargavi Aunt?"

Diravi did not know her, but he knew that his Paatta had had two children by Ammachi, a boy and a girl. The son was Krishnankutty; the daughter Bhargavi...

"Even we don't know much about Aunt Bhargavi. I came to know only now. My mother told me not to tell anyone... Bhargavi ran away from home ten years ago. When young, she used to go to the Palmyra-grove beyond the Valli River. One day, she did not return. We heard that she had run away with the Nadar, the young fellow who climbed coconut trees, and had left for far-off lands."

"Didn't they search for her?" asked Diravi in wonder.

"They did, but could not find her. At that time, Grandfather had fixed a groom for Bhargavi, but she was not willing to marry him it seems." Sasi told Diravi all that he had learnt from his mother. There had been no news of Bhargavi or her Chellan Nadar for a long time. But ten years later, which was now, about eight days ago, she had written to her mother. She was living with her husband at Neyyantinkara. She had a son and a daughter to support. A month ago, the Nadar slipped while climbing a tree and broke his leg; he could no longer exercise his profession. She had written asking for whatever help her mother could provide. It had to be done without her husband's knowledge or he might refuse to accept their help. It was to consult the father of the girl about this that Granny had sent for her old lover and husband. Could she come to a decision without consulting the father of the girl?

Krishnankutty was very angry. "She brought shame upon our family. Why should we help her?" he asked. Grandfather calmed him and told Ammachi, "I can give you a little money. Take it, go and see our daughter, find out where she is, how she is…all things happen as fated. We can help, but little."

Sasi left Diravi after telling him the story. Diravi walked on thinking of the new woman he had heard of that day; it was a face that he did not know of; he had never seen Bhargavi. He suddenly thought of his weeping sister, Nagu, and Bhargavi; they were in a somewhat similar predicament. Though he had felt he had to admire Bhargavi's Nadar husband for not asking his wife's people for help and perhaps even forbidding it. What a contrast this person was to his brother-in-law, who had sent his wedded wife home without any reason!

Fourteen

As far as the eye could see, the fields stretched green on green. When Diravi turned into his street on his way back from school, he saw Koonangani Paatta walking towards him slowly. Unnamalai Aachi herself was past 60; he was 10 years older, but healthy and though quite bald, his looks had a certain majesty; his walk was upright and firm. But the lines on his face showed the bitterness of his life's experiences.

"Eh, you are coming back only now from school. You are tired; you look hungry. Unnamalai is waiting outside for her dear grandson. I am going to see the tenant, Rasaiya," Paatta said in his usual cheerful tone and stepped into the fields. On the way, opposite Khader Tailor's Shop, Andi Pillai Uncle called out, "Eh, Diravi."

Diravi went up to the shop. He was given a paper packet with the words, "Give this to Thayi Aunt; her jumper is ready." Diravi took the parcel. He noticed that Khader and two other people were also in the shop, playing cards; they looked at him in a significant manner.

As he trudged along, Diravi felt that he had to be sympathetic to Koonangani Paatta. Andi Pillai Uncle is three years older than I am. But he is only one class ahead of me. He is to be found in this Khader's shop at all times, playing cards. In his old age, Paatta has to go in search of his tenant. Andi Pillai Uncle had not attended school for many days, but was quite jolly, spending his time playing cards… Diravi sighed. Not just his son, but the other two were also bad. They were his sons, but none of them helped him. Even if the washerman does not come, his two wives would send the old man to the washerman's house, not the sons. All three boys were spoiled by their mothers. It is in the family, Unnamalai Aachi tells me often. Even Mookandi Great-grandfather died because of the behaviour of his son, this Koonangani Paatta. That sin he has to expiate by suffering at the hands of his two wives and his three sons, poor fellow. Can a tiger sire a cat?

Both his mother and Aachi used to tell Diravi stories about his Paatta. Diravi was an expert at making them tell him all that he wanted to know. After his father's death, Koonangani Paatta had lived for five years in Ammachi's house. His affection for Ammachi had kept him steady; he had never looked at another woman. It was said that it was due to her influence that he returned to his family. His mother was determined to get him married and she wore him down. At last, he consented to marry Ponamu on Ammachi's insistence that he should please his mother. Paatta was 30 at that time.

The marriage was not a great success. Ponamu Aachi was from a poor family at Padmanabhapuram. Even after ten years, Koonangani Paatta and Ponamu Aachi had no children. On his mother's death, Paatta's sister, Unnamalai Aachi, arranged for Paatta's second marriage with Ananji Pillai Aachi. After Paatta arrived in Eraniyal with his wives, Ponamu Aachi had three children—Iyavu, Neelapillai and Pitcha Pillai. Ananji Pillai Aachi had twins—Thayi and Andi Pillai. According to all reports, all Koonangani Paatta's sons were skilled at all sorts of devious deeds, like his father in his youth. Nobody listened to what Paatta said; everyone went his or her own way in that house. Frequent quarrels would break out between the rival wives, affecting everyone in the house. People were interested in taking everything he had, never in giving him anything. It was a case of the son beating the father or almost near it. The son's voice was heard all over stacking error street.

Paatta liked Diravi very much. He would often come home and sorrowfully tell Aachi, Father, and Mother the story of his house. Aachi would say, "If we behave properly, so will our children." And he wouldn't allow Aachi to conclude, but would interrupt saying, "You know nothing. There was no one better behaved than our own father. And why was I born a misfit. All this is destiny," he would add philosophically.

Sometimes he would come in, his face dark with anger, "Shouting at them makes my throat dry. Kuttiamma, give me some water." He would take a piece of palm-jaggery in his mouth, drink a tumbler of water, and lie quietly on the outer verandah. "Children should not be told about the behaviour of their father when young; they will not grow up to respect him," he would say, following his own secret thoughts. Sometimes, he sounded incoherent.

When Diravi entered the corner street, some girls were playing hopscotch. On the verandah of Thayi Aunt's house two girls were playing with round stones. He went into the house to see Thayi Aunt who was wearing a deep red sari. He gave her the jacket, which Andi Pillai had given him. Thayi aunt's husband had a shop of indigenous medicines in the market—roots, plants, leaves, branches etc. The house smelt strongly of native herbs. Uncle usually came back at 4 from the shop for his meal. He had eaten and was stretched out on a bench inside. Uncle's mother, Sembi Atha[1] was in the backyard, underneath the coconut palm, cleaning some fish. Her hands were bloody and about her lay fish scales shining in the evening light. A cat was ready to spring on what was offered it from time to time. It was otherwise busy driving off the crows that came to share the repast. The pot was full of bright fish eyes staring starkly. The stink of fish drowned the smell of native medicines and herbs.

Washing her hands, Atha noticed Diravi and called out, "Is it Diravi? Why are you standing dumbly behind?"

Thayi Aunt shouted, "Eat your meal with us tonight; there is good fish for you. It came too late for the noon meal..."

"We don't eat fish these days," replied Diravi. "I don't even know how to remove the fish bones." He was about to leave, when Aunt called him into the kitchen. The stove was burning brightly. Her eyes reflected the light of the stove. She lifted the cast iron vessel from the oven, gripping it with a towel. There was a pleasant smell of pepper and garlic.

Diravi never tired of watching Thayi Aunt's face; he stood watching her now. She drew the burning logs of wood from the stove and drenched them with water. She prepared to grind the masala, her legs conveniently gripping both sides of the grinding stone. Watching her, Diravi was lost in his own thoughts wondering what she would ask him.

"What was decided about Nagu Akka?" she eventually inquired.

"Nothing happened. Things are exactly as they were..."

She finished and took what she had ground to the stove and Diravi followed. Her mother-in-law came in with the cleaned fish and said to Diravi, "But this Papathi should not be allowed to get away with it...she should be... But she even put aside her own husband. Poor innocent Nagu. If it had been you, my daughter-in-law, you would have driven Papathi out of her house. Don't I know you?" began the mother-in-law. The mustard in the pot on the oven popped in rhythm with her words.

They met in a regular battle. The child in the cradle began to weep loudly amidst the noise of the quarrel. The cat was the victim of a kick by Aunt and added its screech to the din. Diravi wanted to escape and went out. But before he reached the street, he could hear his uncle, Kolappa Pillai, awakened by the noise of the quarrel, talking gruffly to his mother, "You are a dying woman. Why don't you keep quiet? You are grey but are still like a dog, always ready for a quarrel.

She is young and unwisely says something. Why should you reply to it? I have told you a thousand times you are a buffalo who doesn't feel the rain. If you do not keep quiet, I'll throw you out."

Diravi did not hear what else he said. But this was customary in that house. That pitiful creature, the mother of his uncle… Aunt would draw her out into a quarrel and the son would take the mother to task, invariably abusing her and promising to push her out. This was a daily event in that house. Diravi's uncle was henpecked… Why should he be like that, wondered Diravi. People said that he had once or twice beaten his own mother, abetted by his wife. But Diravi did not know whether it was true. He would call his mother "Hey" as if he were calling the servant. That was why Aunt was the way she was.

How different this Kolappa Uncle was from that Sevantha Perumal Pillai! Diravi sighed.

Fifteen

Things were coming to normalcy after Nagu Akka had been thrown out of her husband's house. Time is a healing factor one cannot reckon with. Things went on as usual, but the problem of Nagu Akka lingered in everyone's mind. Yet even, she had come to accept her fate and had begun voluntarily to attend to household chores. She swept the house and backyard clean as if her whole life depended on it; she would not notice that the water tub was full and would go on drawing bucket after bucket from the well, adding to the tub even when it overflowed. If she had nothing else to do, she would dry the paddy and begin to husk it. She seemed driven to work continuously in an effort to forget her own plight.

Mother's face was frozen in her sorrow. Father grew more and more silent. Gone were the days when he enjoyed gossiping with his mother and wife. He was either silent, or quarrelling with Mother for every trivial reason. Something was always wrong—the sacred ash was not replenished in the receptacle, or there was too much salt in the rasam[1] or too little in the boiled vegetable… Unnamalai Aachi exploded from time to time abusing that sinful woman Papathi, saying, "If this continues, what shall we do? We have to do something." When she said this once to Father, he shouted, "What shall I do? Shall I kill myself?"

Aachi never liked any talk of death. With a tone of great resignation, she would reply, "Those who are going to die will die. Are we going to preserve them in oil? All of us have to die one day..."

The only person who was, as it were, unaffected by all this was Visalam. She went on as usual, often worrying Aachi for a story in the evening or early in the morning. And untiringly, Aachi would repeat to her the story of the simpleton who went to his mother-in-law's place and made a fool of himself... All these stories wearied Diravi, who had heard them many number of times from the same source. These days, he was not particularly interested in listening to Aachi's stories.

Life was interesting and went on in its humdrum way. Days went by—but who can stop buying and selling and eating and drinking. It was Diravi's duty to go to the Monday market and buy a rupee's worth of vegetables for the week. One Monday, he was returning with a bag of vegetables when he was called by Brother-in-law Sevantha Perumal's father, Kannu Pillai. He had covered himself with a cloth from head to foot and was sitting in the sun, warming himself in the house of the Krishna woman.

"Eh Diravi, come here," he called. The old fellow's face was swollen in places; his forearms had thickened with disease. His fingers had withered at the tips. His eyes were streaming.

He he was like a boil about to burst. He said, "Don't think that I am trying to open old wounds. I heard all about it." While he was saying it, Lakshmi Atha, his present Krishnakari wife, came adorned up to her elbow with cowdung with which she had evidently been working and said, "Who is it? Diravi? I thought it was someone else."

This woman supported the family by maintaining two or three buffaloes and cows. She was old, completely grey, and wore no blouse. She wore a magenta sari and smelt of buffaloes. Diravi stood looking at the buffaloes in the barn. Kannu Pillai then went on, "Your father should be blamed for marrying his parrot-like daughter to that killer fellow…" He was blaming Father for having given his daughter in marriage to a fellow who had driven his own father from his home and livelihood. It was a mistake.

"But who could have expected these things to happen?" Lakshmi Atha said.

"When he drove me out of my home, taking his mother's side, I kept thinking that God would give him his due… I am an old fellow; my days are done. But the girl Nagu is young; she has not even been married six months. Can we allow things to continue like this?"

A fit of coughing interrupted him. His eyes almost popped out with the effort. He spat and continued. Hearing the sound of a buffalo overturning something, Lakshmi Atha ran inside cursing the animal.

"Tell your father that I told you this. He should not leave it at this. Ask him to make a complaint in the court against my son. I will also join him in the complaint. I do not know for what sins in my past life I now suffer from this disease. Neither dog nor ghost comes near me now, but he…he is my son. I can't refrain from saying what I have to say. I do not know what the fellow will suffer from in his next life, or tomorrow itself. A green leaf laughs at a brown leaf, they say…"

He could not speak any more; he choked with emotion and panted heavily. All his limbs shook. Diravi could not stay there longer. He felt like weeping before he left.

When he reached home, Diravi saw Father and neighbour Annamalai Pillai talking. He told them what Kannu Pillai had told him. Annamalai Pillai added, "You should not keep quiet, Nagaru Pillai. Even his father says to go to court. Let us!"

Father did not reply. His face, these days, bore an expression of great pain. "How can we benefit by going to court?" he asked resignedly.

"We can teach Sevantha Perumal Pillai a lesson. This bluster will not serve him in court. The lawyer will make him reveal his secret and punish him."

"Our *vakil*[2] will lay bare his secrets. But his *vakil* will lay bare our Nagu's secrets…"

"But what has Nagu to fear? Unless you have a wound in your back, why should you be afraid to bend? If there is anything in the pot, the ladle will bring it up. When there is nothing…"

"I asked *vakil*'s clerk, Krishnan Kutty, about this and he said that if we go to court, there will be some sparks, but practically no remedy for this. If either husband or wife is dissatisfied with the spouse, there is no law of the land to keep them together. If a case is instituted, then both would have to live apart permanently; there will then be no reconciliation possible at any time. And it will be a costly one, this business of going to court. *Vakils* and witnesses will demand money. And if we win the case, we might get a little maintenance money from the husband—nothing more. Will it soothe my daughter's painful memories? Would she be consoled with a little money? Would we be satisfied? Our affairs will be talked about by the town a little more—that is all..."

Aachi came to the container of sacred ash, took a liberal handful, applied it to her forehead and stepped down into the courtyard to glance at the sun and recite the prescribed mantras.[3] Her son's last sentence reached her and she said, "If we do nothing, how long is the girl to grieve like this? And should we bear it?"

"You are the only one in this house who is affected by her sorrows, isn't it? Are the rest of us happy about it? Let me go and take Sevantha Perumal Pillai by the hand and bid him take the girl home—he will do it, immediately, won't he? Father was both annoyed and hurt. He was perspiring profusely. Annamalai Pillai tried to work peace between mother and son before they quarrelled anymore. Aachi said, I am sorry. You do what you like. Why should I interfere with my impractical ideas and be abused? I am only waiting for God to call me before, I see worse things than this..." Her eyes were full of tears and she retired to a corner of the house, stood in the bright sun and prayed with eyes closed.

Whenever talk turned to Nagu Akka's problem, it always ended in Aachi's tears. But she could not keep quiet about it for more than two days, when invariably she would again quarrel with her son about it. Once Father said, "Two hands have to clap to create a sound. Let us keep quiet a little while. The fellow might change his mind and take Nagu back... even our astrologer has held out this hope to me..." That day, the talk ended there. Father had to go to buy some seedlings and he was away for a while.

In a few days, the vessels and things that had been sent with Nagu Akka to her husband's house were returned by Papathi Ammal, in small lots, but not all of it; only a part of what was given was returned. But no one wanted to quarrel about it as Papathi and her son had quarrelled about getting them cast aside by her husband and no one was interested in claiming what was given as dowry. In fact, we tried to prevent anything being returned, but there was no stopping what came back. Aachi would murmur something and be supported by Mother—Father wouldn't even be present. What a huge collection of things had been given as dowry at Nagu Akka's wedding. Brass vessels, plates of coir, wood, metal, and other materials, ladles of wood as well as of brass and other metals, boxes, brooms—how much did it all weigh? Sweets, containers with sweets...there was even a complaint that the sweets meant to be distributed by Papathi in the town were not distributed. God knew what had happened to all the sweets that were given. Father had given away money with each ceremony. And then oil, two bags of the best rice, and grains and pulses, two sacks of coconuts, four hundred weights of mutton, salt, pepper, other masalas[4] along with ten rupees in cash…

Diravi remembered a number of things. Onam[5] had come within a few weeks of the wedding. It was the bridal pair's first Onam. For every person in the groom's house, Father bought new clothes, sweets, and other things. We are not Malayalis, but Papathi insisted that we bring the traditional Onam gifts. Father, afraid to quarrel with Papathi, bought new clothes even for her brothers and their wives. Father had no money left ot buy Salam any good clothes. His own family had to make do with cheap stuff.

As days passed, Diravi's mind was only occasionally immersed in matters of the past in connection with his Nagu Akka's wedding. But at the bottom of his mind gathered a great hatred for Papathi and Sevantha Perumal, and the community which allowed them to live as respectable citizens in their midst. He was getting angrier and angrier.

Sixteen

News came from Pazhavadai that Sister Unnamalai was expecting a child. Aachi was sure that the news was the result of the wasps having built a nest behind the front door of the house; she said that whatever the confusion at home we have to do the right thing by our daughter. It is her first. She has conceived a long time after marriage."

In the fifth month, they began making eats for the expectant mother. They had to make five different kinds, as that was the usual thing. Father begged and borrowed the required amount of money from many people. What would the town say if things were not done properly?

The five kinds of eatables were ready and Father, Mother, and Salam went to visit their first daughter. As soon as they returned, Unnamalai Aachi inquired anxiously. "Eh Kuttiamma! How is my granddaughter? Did she have much nausea?"

"It was severe. She could not raise her head. She has grown thin, with insufficient food. Even this morning, before we left, she was saying she felt sick. We wanted to bright her home with us, but her father-in-law asked for her to be left with them till the *seemantham*[1] ceremony in two months' time. After that, we can bring her here," replied Mother.

Diravi regretted not having gone with them to Pazhavadai. He had not been there for a long time. But school kept him back.

Brother-in-law was a decent and good natured man. He was very light skinned and called a "white man" by many in fun. Diravi had seen two white people. When Aiyavu Uncle was ill with jaundice, he had gone with Father to the hospital in Nayyoor where he had seen a nun. Only here, fair faces with rosy skin was visible; she wore a white dress and had catlike eyes. Father said that she was a white woman, a virgin, unmarried.

And then, once when the Maharaja was visiting Eraniyal, he was part of the crowd that had stared at the Maharaja from a distance. With the Maharaja was a white man, rosy to the eye. The boys came back to school and asked their teacher, Govindarama Iyer, about it. He said, "In Europue, all men and women are of that colour."

Diravi was not sure how his brother-in-law acquired the same colour as Europeans. When he saw him for the first time, he asked Unnamalai Aachi, "How is he this colour? Were his father and mother white?"

Aachi prevented him from probing any further and told him, "His parents were as black or brown as all of us."

It was Koonangani Paatta who solved Diravi's problem for him one day. They had gone to attend a wedding and there he saw two extremely light skinned people. He asked Paatta about it, "Oh foolish fellow; these things happen. My father and mother were very fair but I am dark. Your father and mother are dark, but you are fair. Salam is your sister, but she is dark."

This was chance; one in a thousand was born fair in colour. This was all God's will and sport, according to Koonangani Paatta.

Diravi remembered that Brother-in-law's eyes were almost always half closed, as if they were afraid of the light. But he did not need glasses to read. He was the reader of the puranas[2] in the Pazhavadai Vinayaka temple. *Tiruppugazh, Tiruvembavai, Ramayanam, Mahabharatham*[3]—he read these with great charm and earned his livelihood by them.

Diravi had not liked him at first. But compared to Sevantha Perumal, he was a gem of a man. He would bring something for Diravi, whenever he came visiting. If Sister Unnamalai came with him, she would bring the kind of sweets and savouries that he liked best. The gruel she made, from the flour she brought, was always tasty. Similarly, when he left Eraniyal, Pazhavadai Brother-in-law would not forget to give Diravi a coin. A *chakram* coin was a beautiful thing. Heavy and smooth. On one side was the head of the Maharaja, as if cut off by a sword. On the other, the words *One Chakram*[4] *Travancore Rajyam*[5]. The coin would smell of snuff, because Brother-in-law always used snuff.

Two months afterwards, when Diravi came from school he heard that Unnamalai Sister's *seemantham* ceremony was fixed for the following Monday. There were seven eatables to be made now, and they would all go to Pazhavadai and would bring Sister home for her delivery. Father sold paddy and brought some money; things were bought and necessary eatables, both sweet and savoury, made in plenty. It was to be distributed among the townspeople also, so a lot of it was made.

But poor Nagu Akka; no one seemed to have the time to worry about her affairs now. Even she had no time to think of her sorrows; she ran about doing so much of the work.

Brother-in-law had sent invitations to everyone in the family. It was said that an invitation had been sent even to Sevantha Perumal. If Nagu Akka had been living with her husband, she too would have come with him for her sister's *seemantham*. Now she was left in the care of Unnamalai Aachi. All the rest of them set out for Pazhavadai—including Koonangani Grandpa, his wives, Thayi Aunt, all of whom carried gifts for Sister.

Two cartloads of people. It was a delightful journey though bumpy, heads knocking on the roof of the carts on the uneven roads. The older men walked alongside the carts. When they got tired they would get in. The moonlight was mellow and cool. The palms sounded on both sides of the path in the wind. It was about twelve miles to Pazhavadai and a pleasant journey it was.

Because his legs went to sleep, Diravi too got off the cart and walked along with his Father for a little distance. The palm fronds sounded like strange trumpets; the moonlight cast interesting shadows through the palm leaves. Palm fruit fell with a thud and, when Diravi ran to take them, Ponamu Aachi bawled out, "Ghosts rest on palm fruits. Before you pick it up, spit loudly and drive the ghosts away." Diravi obeyed her instructions. He had tasted palm fruit and found it quite palatable.

They reached Sister's house in Pazhavadai early in the morning. There were many relatives who had come not only from the town, but from other places also. Subbu Pillai Grandfather, Nagammai Aachi, Brother-in-law's brother, his wife and children, and many others had come for the ceremony. Brother-in-law had lost his mother and, so, every woman present treated him like a son. There was his father, Iyyam Pillai, who lived with him, rushing here and there, busily attending to many things. He was happy at the prospect of the birth of a grandchild and told Diravi, "You are going to be an uncle, young fellow."

Pipes and drums were playing merrily. Unnamalai Akka, bathed, and wearing a big red mark on her forehead, stepped out in a new silk sari and sat on the platform. Diravi felt proud of her. How charming she looked; she had filled out very slightly. The women stood round Akka and teased her. They were all laughing happily. The platform was filled with presents, eatables, and vessels, which the guests had brought. Mother said, "Your brother-in-law attends all the weddings and other occasions in town and takes presents for them. So, no one has forgotten him now; all of them have brought gifts for him." Diravi could see that both his parents were proud of the occasion, the show and the pomp.

The bangle-seller came in the meantime and adorned his sister's forearms with dazzling sets of bangles. All the women and girls also received bangles, much to their satisfaction.

Koonangani Paatta hurried them. "By 2, the auspicious hour will be over. We have to take her home to Eraniyal. At least, commence at a good time."

Iyam Pillai Uncle loudly invited everyone to the feast, which was excellent. Diravi sat next to his brother-in-law. Many rows of guests partook in the feast.

When the first batch of men finished eating, Iyam Pillai Uncle invited the women among the guests to form the next batch. The women had their food and then Father gave money in a betel leaf roll to his son-in-law sitting on the platform. Neither Iyam Pillai not brother-in-law counted the money. Everything went smoothly. The women sang *kolavai*. The assembled elders scattered sacred ash as a sign of their blessing. Then they tied a piece of each of the eatables in a knot in Unnamalai Akka's sari.

The husband was told that he should not see his wife leaving; they bade him go and wait in the barn. He turned to look at his wife. Diravi thought that he was close to tears. He left for the barn.

To the cheerful and noisy singing of *kolavai*, Akka made obeisance to her father-in-law, touched his feet, and put her hands to her eyes. "Go child, and come back with a babe in your arms," blessed the old man.

Everyone took leave of one another. They had engaged a spring axle cart specially for Sister.

Diravi ran to the barn to take leave of his brother-in-law. His face was as red as a hibiscus flower; and he had a kind of unseeing look in his eyes. "You are ready to go. In four or five days, I shall be there in your house. Tell your Akka also," he said. Diravi felt sorry him; Brother-in-law would now have to live away from his dear wife for some months.

Everyone had got into the carts and were ready to go. Diravi ran to the driver's seat of the cart with the spring axle and sat with the driver. Akka did not speak to him, but was sunk in her own thoughts.

"Akka," Diravi ventured. She did not reply.

"Akka..."

"Yes."

"Brother-in-law said…"

"Yes."

"He said that he will come to Eraniyal in four or five days. He wanted me to tell you, so that you would not miss him."

Unnamalai Akka laughed. And Diravi began to talk of his school, studies, and other things. In the carts following, people were gossiping merrily about all kinds of interesting things. Everyone was happy.

Suddenly, Diravi remembered his Nagu Akka. What would she be doing now? Would she be weeping with anxiety, hoping for her own *seemantham* ceremony? Pity. She was also his sister. He was overcome by pity; thoughts of his Nagu Akka began to haunt him now.

Seventeen

It was late in the night when the party reached Eraniyal. Diravi did not even want to eat and went straight to bed.

He woke to the sound of someone weeping. Someone was abusing someone else. He heard people arriving. The sound of footsteps as they left. There seemed to be a crowd gathering in the street.

Was it a dream? Or was it all really happening? His eyelids were heavy. Somehow, he forced himself to wake up and sit up in bed. It was broad daylight; the sun was shining brightly. The first thing he saw was his father sitting on the front platform his face covered with both hands.

Someone was weeping inside…yes…it was the sound of Nagu Akka weeping. He could hear Unnamalai Akka trying to say something to console her.

Aachi and Mother were shouting together. Inside stood some of the women of the neighbourhood. Mother's face was set in deep sorrow. Salam was nowhere to be seen.

Diravi got up, asking himself what had happened. He was both sad and frightened. Why was Father sitting motionless like this? As he was turning to go inside, a voice was heard, "What is this, Nagaru Pillai?" It was Annamalai Pillai, the neighbour, entering the house. His father looked up; his eyes were red as if he had been weeping. A tremor went through Diravi. Hearing the neighbour's voice, the women emerged from the house.

"It has happened. What can we do about it. What we have heard is true."

"How murderous those people are!" exclaimed Aachi.

"When did it happen?" asked Mother.

"Only this morning at 5 o'clock. In secret, that worst of women, Papathi, and that sinful brute, along with their new bride's parents, went to Velli Malai and celebrated the wedding, it seems. Now, it will be 8. The *thali* was tied an hour ago. They are also back now..."

Annamalai Pillai was panting with the exertion of running. Mother asked, "No one, even in Puthan Street, knew of it?"

"Not even their neighbour, Iyappan Pillai, knew anything about it."

"Who expected that Ekkimatan Pillai and his wife, Bhoomu, would do something like this? Even if they have many grown-up daughters, should one of them be sacrificed like this? He did not even tell us..." Aachi's helplessness was clear.

"This was the reason for Ekkimatan supporting Mookan in the beginning. Now it is clear. He is really a worm, a termite. What a marriage he has arranged! It is time he came to an end, sinful soul that he is!"

Diravi was now sure that it was not a dream, but dire reality. Brother-in-law Sevantha Perumal had secretly married the first daughter of Ekkimatan Pillai. That was it. What would happen to Nagu Akka? The sorrow that had been consuming them slowly had come to a head; there was no turning back now. Diravi's anger boiled over. He could not contain himself.

The head-shaking old woman, Koonangani Paatta, Ponamu Aachi, Ananji Pillai Aachi, and a number of others had gathered in the courtyard. With one voice, they cursed Papathi and Sevantha Perumal, her son. Over all this noise could be heard the weeping of Nagu Akka—it was the weeping of a helpless child. It wrung the heart of everyone who heard. Father sat like a stone, unmoving. Suddenly he said, "Come Nagammai. I will take you to your husband's house. Let us see what he does now. I didn't want to make a public show of my sorrow. We should not allow things to remain as they are. Is there no justice in this town?"

Diravi had never seen his father so angry. Everyone supported Father. And Nagu Akka came out ready to follow her father to her husband's house. Her face was swollen with weeping. "No one need come with us. I shall take her alone to her husband's house and leave her there and come back," said.Father and, placing a towel on his shoulder, stepped into the street. Nagu Akka followed him, with his head down. Diravi was sorry to see his sister so broken-hearted. What had she not suffered in the last few days!

Everyone assembled was worried about what would happen at her in-laws' house. Time dragged by. If Father were to get into a fight with the fellow...

The head-shaking old woman observed, "What a story this is! Evidently, the evil age of Kali[1]—these things happen. What is wrong with this charming girl, Nagu? If he needed another woman, why didn't he marry her openly? Why should he go like a thief at night and get married away from home and town; I was the third wife of my husband. What was wrong with me? Everything was done openly, without fear or favour in the town. This stinks up the Chetti families of Eraniyal…something is rotten..."

The women were talking among themselves. Diravi was watching anxiously, and saw Father at the end of the street, walking as briskly as he had set out, "Father is back," he shouted.

Father arrived and sat on the fore verandah. Having walked rapidly, he was perspiring profusely. He was panting with exertion and could not speak for a while.

"He is perspiring all over. Come Salam, fan him," ordered Aachi. While Salam came to fan him, she could not contain her anxiety and asked, "Did you leave her there in her husband's house?"

"Yes, I left her there." He sighed. "He shouted and made a lot of noise. I too got angry. I left the girl in his presence and spoke two sentences."

"What did you say?" asked Annamalai Pillai.

"Nothing more than—"This is your wife, what you do with her is your affair." I did not say anything else."

"Didn't the mother-in-law say anything? Didn't she see you?"

"She did! She did! But I did not listen to all that she was saying. I was very angry; I shouted, but I do not remember what I shouted in my anger."

"Was the second wife also there?" Ananji Pillai Aachi asked the question that interested her.

"She was," Father replied angrily.

Throughout the day in the street and in the town, this was the talk. "Poor fellow! What else could he do? One should be temperate; even a cow will attack you, if you tease it too much." Diravi was satisfied that the townspeople thought that what his Father had done was right.

Kuttalam was now working in a shop; weighing things in the Monday market. As he had promised, he had left school. He bought tapioca in lots and sold it to those who needed it in smaller quantities. When he next met Diravi, he said, "It is good that your Father found the courage to do what he did. All these fellows should be taught such lessons. I shall get at Perumal one of these days. I am waiting for an opportunity. I shall teach him a lesson, I shall beat him till he cries for mercy!"

Ekkimatan Pillai and his wife, Bhoomu, were proud of what they had done, marrying their eldest daughter into a rich family. Suddenly, they saw themselves as persons of some importance. Their boy, Velappan, who always had a runny nose, began to wear new earrings, new clothes, and things indicative of his new status in the community.

Ekkimatan had ten children. The first was Vadivu—she was 18. The third child was Velappan. The others were all girls. He could not feed them all properly. Husband and wife quarrelled incessantly. The problem of Vadivu's marriage had been bothering them; when they found an easy solution. The father-in-law became the accountant in his son-in-law's shop.

Father had left Nagu in their house in a passion, hearing of the second marriage of his son-in-law. But he was unhappy about it all; he did not recover from the blow, nor was he certain that what he had done was right. It was as if he had suffered a permanent loss...everyone in the house felt like that—as if they had lost something. The fellow was rowdy; he might be beating Nagu Akka lifeless for all they knew.

The fishwife, Vellachi, was the first to come with news of Nagu Akka. She was the newspaper in which all the secrets of all the households were published. She was an uncouth figure, but a sincere jolly woman who spoke with her arms flying about, breasts bouncing inside her loose jumper, as if they were long pestles, and her hips rotating as she walked... she was a sight to see. Women would flock around her as soon as she gave voice, both to buy fish and to listen to the secrets she had to make public. She would hawk her fish with, "This fish is of the first quality from the ocean of milk."

What she could not say in public, she would say in private, seeking out the parties she wanted. She brought news of Nagu Akka to Diravi's house one day. Mother gave Vellachi the gruel, which she drank, making ugly noises. Her teeth were yellow and all of them were visible. She asked, "Why do you leave your daughter with that demoness?"

"What is it, Vellachi? What is happening to Nagu?" Mother enquired fearfully.

"She has neither food nor gruel. She is badly treated..."

"Tell me quickly all that you have to say," Mother said impatiently.

"Her husband also beats her cruelly!"

This news spread slowly throughout the street. When the rumour was confirmed by some others who had heard Nagu Akka being beaten till she wept, everyone at home was angry and exasperated. Unnamalai Aachi began to urge Father. "Eh Dorai! Did we bring up our girl for 15 years for that bastard to beat to death? Even the crow thinks of its young as golden. Go and bring her back. We'll make her comfortable in our house as long as she lives. She does not need a husband. What would we have done if our daughter had become a widow? Now, bring her back to be with us."

But Father was not satisfied with that solution. 'Why talk like this? You talked and drove me to take her back to that house. Now you want me to bring her back. I know that they are up to all sorts of things—they might even kill her. Let them kill her. Your tongue is long and useless!"

But Father's eyes filled with tears thinking of his daughter being beaten by that fool. Poor Father! What was he to do, thought Diravi. Aachi and Mother were constantly at Father to bring Nagu back. In his anger, Father abused everybody. He never stayed at home and did not eat properly.

Nothing was right in the house. In all this hullabaloo, Unnamalai Akka was expecting her firstborn. She also wept, lying down at all hours of the day and night.

In the meantime, elder Brother-in-law, Thapasi Pillai, Iyam Pillai Uncle and Sister-in-law came to see Unnamalai Akka as was expected. They came with sweets and eatables. And no matter how sorrowful the house, one had to attend properly to guests. But talk of Nagammai could not be avoided and Sister Unnamalai's husband offered to go and see Sevantha Perumal and try to talk to him. But he returned before long, all red and stammering. He too suggested that Nagu Akka be brought back.

Father was sad and restless on hearing the words of his elder son-in-law. There was again sorrow in the house. Suddenly, Father went to the well and made a lot of noise drawing water, washing his feet, face, and hands. Where was he going? Was it to Puthan Street to bring Nagu Akka back?

It was 8:30 in the morning. Father had not yet left. Before the house stood the spring axle cart of Sevantha Perumal Pillai. Sevantha Perumal got down, jumping angrily from the cart. He dragged a weaker, frailer Nagu, a quarter of her former size from the cart. She was weeping, but without the strength to weep. Perumal dragged her into the house and said to Aachi who advanced angrily, 'We don't want this person who is neither man nor woman to die in our house. We are not going to bear witness to her death. If she wants to commit suicide, let her do it here. Don't send her back to my house. If you do, we will not be responsible for what happens."

He shouted angrily, pushed Nagu Akka into the courtyard, and left in a hurry.

Eighteen

In a few days, everything about this episode was known to everyone else. Nagu Akka, unable to bear the painful thrashings and the pangs of starvation, had tried to commit suicide by hanging herself from the crossbeam in Perumal's back verandah. Papathi, who saw her, prevented Nagu from putting an end to it all. It was all very upsetting and, the next moment, Sevantha Perumal had taken her back to her parental home. Philosophically, Aachi consoled Nagu, "Consider that fellow dead. Be happy," she advised. And because of Unnamalai Akka, who tried to be cheerful in the house, even Nagu Akka recovered some of her spirits.

Neighbours often came to see Unnamalai Akka who was carrying. One night Unnamalai Aachi hurried everybody. She asked Salam and Diravi to eat early. She drove Father to the shop to get some margosa oil and some other medicines. "Kuttiamma, you will be a grandmother before the night is out. And Diravi will become an uncle..."

There was a lot of going and coming in the house. Both Diravi and Salam were unable to sleep. Ponamu Aachi and Ananji Pillai Aachi came running, on hearing about it. Unnamalai Akka lay moaning with pain. The women were all running about busily inside. Father sat unmoving. He was worried.

Diravi did not know when he fell asleep. But he came awake when a newborn babe squealed in the night. He saw Aachi rushing out, announcing the birth of a boy to Unnamalai. She was grinning from ear to ear.

Father too was laughing happily. Mother came out and said, "Make a note of the time for the horoscope."

"The gun was fired just now in the palace. It is 1 o'clock."

"It was Poorattathi[1] yesterday; if it is 1, it is Uttarattathi[2], it is a good day and a good star," said Aachi and went in. Diravi too was glad with a joy he did not fully understand. A new guest in the family. Let his coming make the family forget Nagu's troubles and be happy for a while. He wanted to see his nephew, but fell asleep again. The house was full of the smell of margosa oil being heated.

When he got up in the morning, it was already bright daylight. He ran inside and looked at the little boy. Next to Unnamalai Akka lay a red, rat-like thing, as if dipped in blood. Diravi was secretly repelled.

The household was full of voices and sounds. All the women of the street and neighbouring streets came to see the mother and child. Tapasi Pillai, the child's father, was informed by wire of the new arrival. Every visitor brought presents. And later, Brother-in-law, his father, Iyam Pillai, and two or three women relatives of his, came carrying pepper, garden turmeric, betel leaves, nuts, plantains, and sugar as gifts. These are customary when the first child is born.

Diravi and Salam distributed the plantains and the sugar to all the houses in the street. Akka would be free of the pollution of child-bearing only after she had "touched the pots"[3]. It was only after that that the father could carry the child, Brother-in-law was told. He tried to control his happy laughter, looking alternately at his wife and child.

There was a festival at the Pazhavadai temple at which Brother-in-law's presence was obligatory and he had to leave the next day.

Now a calm crept over Diravi, when he went to school or stayed home. He could see that the others in the house were also quite contented. The child's looks improved; it was not so repulsive any more. With curly hair and eyes like marbles, he was a charming fellow, quite fair skinned. Diravi sat on the floor and Aachi placed the child in his lap. "Don't let the neck fall forward," warned Aachi. Diravi was careful. The child smiled at something.

"His complexion is not like that of your husband. He is of your colour," said Aachi to Unnamalai Akka. Aachi never forgot to give the child its digestive medicine. Unnamalai Aachi would put the child in its hammock of cloth and sing, in a tune peculiar to herself, all the lullabies she knew.

The milk is on the oven;
The child is in the cradle ...
Did you weep for milk?

With eyes darkened
With tilak of gold on the forehead
Fed with milk before it was dusk ...

She sang endlessly in her cracked voice. Whether the child slept or not, Diravi felt sleepy hearing the lullabies his Aachi sang.

Unnamalai Akka was scheduled to "touch the pots" on the 16th day after her delivery. This fact with the day and date, was stated in all the letters Father wrote to relatives. From Pazhavadai, Brother-in-law, his father, and their womenfolk came for the ceremony. From Padmanabhapuram came Mother's parents, Subbu Pillai Paatta, and Nagammai Aachi. From Kulachal came Mother's brother, Pandaram Pillai Uncle, and his wife Ammalu, and their 10-year-old daughter, Kozhalamangai (usually called Kuzhali) in their car.

All of them, instead of enquiring about Unnamalai Akka and her child were more interested in the story of Nagu Akka and what had happened to her. In a single voice they abused Sevantha Perumal for having put Nagu aside and shamelessly marrying another girl. They were all very sympathetic towards Nagu Akka.

Diravi referred to his Mother's father as Pappanapuram Paatta.

Subbu Pillai, as he was known, was a man of great influence in the community. He had defied his community early in life, being the first to seek and secure a government job. He was also a member of the Travancore Dewaswom[4]

Board. He had served as one of its secretaries and, after retirement, was drawing a pension from the Dewaswom Board which was a government body. He dressed well in white and wore wooden sandals. He was bald, had a sandal paste mark on his forehead and always carried a walking stick. He wore a white collarless shirt and wound a long upper cloth round his neck. He spoke so as to display his knowledge of Sanskrit, Malayalam, and Tamil, though some complained that he and his like murdered all three languages. He was still a significant figure. While in service, his field had been enormous. He had served in all the temples in Travancore state in Kanyakumari, Suchindram, Keralapuram, Kumarakovil, Tiruvattaru, Kuzhithurai, Neyyattinkara, Parasalai, Trivandrum, Vaikom, Kaduthurutti, Sabarimalai, Ettumanur, and all the other places that one could name. No matter who the listener or what the conversation, he would immediately begin to talk about temples. "In Arnablapuzha," he would say, "they give the best milk payasam[5]. Even in Trivandrum, they don't make its equal. Its flavour and its taste!" Or he would offer the opinion that if one bathed in Varkalai sea water, one would be cured of all ailments.

He was a simple, innocent man. Even those who did not know him had heard a rather famous story about him. There was, when he was in charge of the area, a complaint about a poor piper who was paid by the Dewaswom to play in a village Bhagavati[6] temple. It was said in the complaint that the piper drew payment for the piper, drummer, *singhi*[7], and the accompanist. As secretary, Subbu Pillai went on a surprise visit to the Bhagavati temple one evening. As soon as he saw the secretary, the piper beat the drum, played the pipe, played the singhi for a while, and then, played the accompaniment, all by turn. Subbu Pillai -was really impressed by the fellow's all round performance. "He deserves all the four salaries he gets; he is doing four persons' work at once," he wrote in answer to the complaint.

Diravi did not know whether the story was wholly true, but he couldn't help laughing whenever he recalled the account. After he was pensioned off, he settled with his wife Nagammai Aachi in Padmanabhapuram. Nagammai Aachi was known for her ingenuity. In driving servants to work and in extracting the best from them, she was unequalled. She was also very sharp-tongued. Wherever Grandfather went, he would say, "Unless I drink a cup of strong tea, such as my wife makes, I cannot sleep soundly at night," and would return in the night to Padmanabhapuram. The old couple got on well and lovingly together. His only son and five daughters were scattered all over the place and the old couple were alone in their house at Padmanabhapuram, with only a small girl to assist them, to keep them company, and do the house work.

The first of their daughters was Diravi's mother, Kuttiamma; she was married in Eraniyal. The next daughter, Mookkammai, was married in Midalam to a tamarind merchant. The third daughter, Berarni, was married in Tiruvithancode to Paramartha Lingam, a farmer-like father. The fourth daughter, Shunmukam, was married to a contractor, Parakkai Mahalingam. The fifth daughter, Bhagavathi, was married in Pazhavadai to Chockalingam. The last of their children was a boy, Pandaram. He was married to Ammalu in Kulachal. She was very rich and had only an old mother; so, Pandaram stayed with his mother-in-law, taking care of their property and business. He had suddenly become rich. Some said that he dealt 'in milk powder from America. Others were of the opinion that he printed counterfeit currency. But whatever he did, he grew rich suddenly and had a lot of money to do what he pleased with.

Aunt Ammalu was a little crazy, a half-wit, but her defect seemed to have been covered up by her riches. She would not talk to anyone who came visiting. This was an economical state of affairs for her husband. So long as she could not make the coffee, he could escape from offering it to a guest. "Who can make it here; she is not all right. What can I do?" He was a miser. Even his other relatives never went to him for anything.

But all this did not bother the old couple; they had married their daughters, off while Subbu Pillai was still in government service. With his small pension he got a plot of land which enabled him to live quite comfortably. If his son loaned him some money, and was strict about collecting it back, the old man would say that it was the right thing to do. But the mother was sorry that her son was a miser. She would say, "He won't pay the oilman, but he will pay twice the amount to the doctor..." She would curse his close-fistedness without letting her husband hear it.

The only benefit that the old man enjoyed from his son's riches was that wherever the son went, his parents too could go without any expense, in his car. He was proud indeed of that privilege. But he was interested in making the world believe that his son was doing the right thing by him. It was a matter of pride to him that the world should believe this of his rich son.

Kuzhalamangai was a few years younger than Diravi. Nagammai Aachi would wink playfully and tell Diravi, "All this wealth is yours, grandson," implying that he was to marry Kuzhalamangai. It used to make Diravi angry with her.

Between the old couple, their five daughters, and one son was shared all the seven towns' wealth associated with the Seven Towns Chettiar community. The old man himself would say, "It just happened that way. Did we plan it? It was simply fated to be so."

Everything was ready for the ceremony of "touching the pots" by Unnamalai Akka to cleanse herself of the pollution of child-bearing. A new sari, blouse, a shirt, and waist-chain for the child, a cradle, a string bearing the necessary stone and iron ring as talisman to save the child from indigestion, fear and other things. Everything was ready.

In the morning, Unnamalai Akka bathed and wore the new dress her husband had brought her. Her face was stained yellow with turmeric and bright with happiness as the child rested in her arms. Her hair was wet. A pot of water was placed in the courtyard. Aachi told her to put her ring into the water, and while the women around sang the *kolavai* song, she was to take out the ring from the pot of water and carry it thrice to her eyes and to the eyes of the child.

Mother came up with the necessary pepper-chilli mix[8] to drive away the evil eye by circling her tightly-closed fists three times over her daughter's head, before placing the mix in the fire. Then Akka went into the kitchen and was made to touch the new pot kept ready for the purpose. Sister also had to touch other pots in the kitchen till the pollution of childbirth had completely left her, according to custom.

In the central hall, the brass light burned brightly. On a mat spread out sat Brother-in-law facing the east. He had brought a length of red silk and Akka carrying the child, walked towards her husband, while all the women sang *kolavai* and placed the child on his father's lap. Brother-in-law was inexperienced with children and the way he struggled to keep the child erect in his lap was funny. Nor could he prevent the child from urinating.

Brother-in-law's sister-in-law laughed and said, "Now you have indeed become a father." Everyone laughed. Brother-in-law looked foolish, his dhoti soaking wet.

The waist-chain with talismans was wound round the child. Then, with great relief, he handed over the child to his wife. Akka gave the child in turn to all present. Even Diravi was given the child to hold for a minute. "Those who hold a newborn child in their arms on this day acquire the merit of a visit to Benares," said Aachi for the thousandth time that day.

Then, there was the feast with payasam and other things. All the visitors had left for their homes, Sister and Brother-in-law stayed on for a while, and everyone was light of heart and happy. Unnamalai Aachi was doubly happy. She bathed the child regularly with a blood-red medicated oil prepared at home. Placing the child on her outstretched legs, she would bathe it, singing songs she knew from long ago.

Crying Ingu Ingu
Going to the garden
Crying Akku Akku
Going to uncle's house
Parrot grown up on words ...

Listening to Aachi singing, Diravi sensed that he too had been bathed that way, when young and helpless.

Everyone forgot their worries in the smiles of the child. When the child smiled in his sleep, Aachi would say that God was teaching it to drive away the jackals. If he wept in his sleep, her comment was that God had told the child that its mother was dead as a joke. If he hiccupped, his belly was becoming bigger to hold more food. If he vomited, Aachi would quote a proverb "the child that vomits most lives the longest." Aachi had a ready stock of worldly wisdom traditional to our community on the raising of a child.

Forty-one days had to pass, before the mother of a newborn child could go out of the house and into the open. That day, she went to the tank for a bath and came back with a pot of water. Nagu Akka was minding the child and she handed him over to her sister. Mother took a burning faggot turning it thrice one way and thrice the opposite way to avert the evil eye. She made the auspicious red liquid by mixing chunam and turmeric in a plate and showed it thrice to mother and child, putting a spot of the red liquid on her forehead and then poured out the whole thing from the plate before the house.

Diravi was surprised at the number of ceremonies and beliefs which surrounded a birth into this world. Mother and child then went up to the temple gate with the warning from Aachi to be careful lest anything evil by way of omens touched the child and harmed him.

It was a month later that Brother-in-law wrote that he was finding it difficult to manage the cooking. And since Unnamalai Akka was also anxious, Father and Mother hired a spring-axle cart and took her to Pazhavadai and left her there with her child and husband.

Nineteen

The exams were on and Diravi had little time left for other things. He did well in the exams and passed. This year he was in the SSLC[1] class. Father wanted him to pass the SSLC and then get a government job.

"All these years, it was all right. Now, this is the last and most important year. Take care, study well, and pass. After that, I don't have the means to put you through college," Father had often warned him.

Diravi was aware of the situation at home. The sentimental attachments and enmities he had felt were now taking shape as real problems and challenging him to a fight to the finish. Nagu Akka was always lost in household chores. Sometimes, she thought of her lot and was sad. Watching her, Diravi's heart ached for her. What a sad lot hers was! It was a problem, a challenge to him.

Sometimes, he would see Sevantha Perumal about the town. He no longer thought of him as his brother-in-law. He used to avoid him, but these days, he sought to hold that fellow's eyes with his own and tried not to give way to him. He thanked Kuttalam for having given him this courage. It was rumoured in town that Papathi did not get on well with her new daughter-in-law, Vadivu, and that the latter was slowly getting the upper hand over Papathi in their quite frequent bickering. It was said that Vadivu also quarrelled bitterly with her husband. He used to stay away from home, not even returning to eat for days at a stretch, after such quarrels. Somehow, this news consoled Diravi. "Sevantha Perumal deserves it," he told himself. "Nagu Akka lived with him, without any quarrels, never raising her voice. He deserved what he got in Vadivu!" If she and her mother, Bhumu, got together, no one in the town could best them in either talk or a quarrel.

In Koonangani Paatta's house, the rival wives were always quarrelling among themselves, making life miserable for the old man. Ponamu Aachi and her children were on one side; Ananji Pillai Aachi and her children on the other. They often met for the express purpose of quarrelling. But both sides quarrelled with their common enemy, the old man, Koonangani Paatta. Diravi felt that he couldn't stand these people any longer.

The old man was tossed in the storm every day. In the meantime, the scandal about Korami teacher and Neelappillai Aunt had reached the town. It was whispered about now. Koonangani would leave the house as soon as Korami teacher entered it. Thayi Aunt often quarrelled with her mother-in-law and ran away to her mother's house. And that henpecked fellow, her husband, would follow her begging her to go back.

Uncle Iyavu's dubious fame was spreading all over the place. His mother, Ponamu, wanted him to get married.

"Your fool of a son deserves to be married? He has no work. He earns nothing. Why make a girl his victim?" asked his father, earning the ill-will of his wife all the more by his statement. "Should you blame your own children?" Ponamu Aachi asked him, "What are you? What have you been? Think about it," she chastised him. She was aware that her husband went to see his old keep, Ammachi, quite often, and was hinting at it. But Diravi knew that Koonangani Paatta went only to arrange help for his daughter, Bhargavi. For two days, Sasi was not to be seen in school. Diravi went to inquire whether he was ill. Walking along to the house, Diravi found it strangely healing to walk in the garden among the fields. The tops of the palm-trees were bright with sunlight. The breeze blew cool, patterning the water that murmured in the irrigation canals. There was no sound, but that of birds. The shrubs smiled with flowers.

Amminikkutti was bathing near the well, like a grown woman, her body covered with a cloth from neck to toe. She did not notice him and was unconsciously, gracefully, pouring water on her head. Diravi was surprised that she was so well-grown and well-built; she was only two years older than Salam. Only after he stepped into the house did he notice that the house seemed deserted. But someone was lying in the dark. It was Ammachi. She was shaking with fever. Diravi sat near her.

She was suffering from her usual monthly filaria. The temperature would rise sharply, but otherwise the fever was harmless. She would have only warm water for three days. Unnamalai Aachi too used to suffer from this fever.

Sasi's mother looked in from the kitchen and said,

"Diravi, how is your sister?"

"Nagu Akka is quite all right," Diravi replied. There was nothing more to say about her. "Why didn't Sasi come to school these two days? Where is he?" asked Diravi, saying that he had come because he had missed Sasi at school.

Ammachi said, "Two days ago, Sasi went to see his aunt, Bhargavi, at Neyyatinkara. He took some rice for her."

"Did you go and see your daughter that day?" Diravi asked.

"I did. When she wrote that she was suffering, how could I keep away? I went and saw her."

She narrated the state she'd found her daughter in. Her Nadar husband had fallen from a tree and broken his leg and could not do any work or bring home any money. Bhargavi did some work and was trying to make some money to support her two young children. She was working in some tea shops. Ammachi tried to persuade her to return home with her, taking the children along. "How can I leave the father of my children when he is helpless?" she had asked.

Talking of her daughter and her troubles, Ammachi was heartbroken, Ammachi promised to send her what she could from time to time and came away. This was another sorrow for Koonangani Paatta.

When Diravi took leave of them and started for home, the sunlight had disappeared. It was not yet completely dark.

He met Amminikkutti plucking the leaves of the drumstick trees planted as fencing. She was freshly bathed and bright with traces of oil on her body. She looked at Diravi. Diravi looked at her. When she did not say anything, he asked, "Have you forgotten me, Ammini?" .

"Is it Diravi Ettan? Have you just come?" She blushed red. "You were hiding when I came," he said. She drew lines with her toes in the soil and stood silent. At her feet were bright red evening-glory flowers. What a divine colour these flowers had! He had nothing to say. He took leave of her and walked on. He turned back a little later and saw Ammini looking intently at him.

Diravi was flustered and walked away faster. Hiranya's[2] blood was spreading across the sky in the setting sun, which was hidden below the horizon. He went past the garden and had scarcely reached the road, before Kuttalam joined him from behind, pushing his cycle. He was perspiring profusely. In the carrier of the cycle was a half-filled sack.

"Where are you coming from?" Diravi asked Kuttalam.

"I got a sackful of *mochai* gram cheap…I hawked it from house to house. I managed to sell half of it. I have to earn now. Father is struck down with paralysis..." This was news to Diravi. "This past week, he has been bedridden which is why I did not meet you for several days; his right side is completely useless. His mouth is also affected..."

"Didn't you get him any medicine?" Diravi was surprised. "Kuttan Vaidyan[3] took a look at him. He prescribed some oil massage and some liquid to drink. But my father is old; it is not likely to help. Aachi also is in a bad way; she too is old and unable to do any work. We'll be dead long before we reach their age. Till now, she was doing some work cooking and earning some money… Now, even that has stopped. I have to earn for all of us. I have to do a good day's work before I go to bed at night: prepare the gruel and medicine for Father, smear the balm on his leg. I have to see to it that my Aachi has had something to eat and drink".

In Kuttalam's speech, there was endless bitterness and a sense of willing sacrifice. He was pushing the cycle along and walking with Diravi, who was sorry to hear about his friend's plight. It was getting darker every minute. The smell of Kuttalam's perspiration blew him way with the breeze. Kuttalam was not wearing a shirt or an upper cloth, only his dhoti. He was well preserved and strong, though he had no time to spend on his physique. His pockmarked face, his unkempt hair and beard gave him a distinctive appearance. He would not run away from his responsibilities; he had learnt to meet them and bear up under them. Suddenly, Kuttalam said, "Sevantha Perumal and Vadivu are quarrelling all the time. His father Kannu Pillai and his keep Lakshmi are also at one another all day."

"What do they quarrel about?" Diravi was curious.

"Who knows? He was bawling at her: 'You ran away from your husband.' She was bawling at him: 'You were driven away from house with a broom by your wife and son'. It was a grand quarrel which everybody witnessed."

Diravi did not know that Lakshmi Atha had deserted her husband; that was news to him. But Kuttalm knew all that was happening in town. Her husband had known of her relationship with Kannu Pillai, but then they had quarrelled over something and she had left him.

There was a brook on their way. Asking Diravi to wait a little, Kuttalm left the cycle leaning against a tree and washed his face and arms and dried himself with his dhoti before proceeding further. Then he continued, "After the quarrel, he left the house. Lakshmi Atha waited for his return in vain. Anticipating his return, she had prepared the things he liked best, but he did not come back. He was a leper set aside by his own wife; his kept wife was waiting for him with love or whatever it was in spite of his disease. This is life ...I advised her like an elderly man. Told her not to make life more difficult for him, poor fellow."

Diravi was glad that Kuttalam had advised Lakshmi Atha in that manner. He was sorry for Kannu Pillai, the poor old man, sick and driven from his home, all his property seized by an unscrupulous wife and son, but that Lakshmi Atha too deserved some sympathy.

"How is Nagu?" Kuttalam asked.

Because Nagu was younger than Kuttalam, he usually enquired after her, often mentioning her by name. But Diravi felt a little awkward about Kuttalam asking him about it like that. Without replying, he looked for a long moment at his friend. Kuttalam did not look directly at him, but suddenly began to examine the cycle chain and check the air in the cycle tyres. They did not look at each other; Diravi thought that his friend was deliberately avoiding looking at him directly.

"She is all right. She has to find some consolation and she finds it in household work." Without wanting to say anything more about Nagu Akka, he said, turning the talk in another direction, "Isn't this a hired cycle? Don't you have to return it?"

Kuttalam now looked directly at him and said, "Yes, it is hired. I shall have to return it. I shall leave this sack at home and then return the cycle."

Then Kuttalam left for Puthan Street and Diravi turned into his. Without any tangible reason, Diravi felt the weight of his burden and worry increase. He felt that a cobra was spreading its hood to cover him and his thoughts, many of which were not clear to him.

Twenty

As usual, Father was in trouble—not having enough seeds to plant. What he had in reserve he sold to someone who had said he needed it; as always, Father urgently needed the cash. And now he had no seeds. "Funeral-licker" Sankara Pillai had bought it from father.

Funeral-licker Sankara Pillai was so called because he made a speciality of walking away with betel leaves and nuts kept for distribution among visitors when there were deaths in the community. He stole when he thought no one was looking, but his thievery was common knowledge and so he was called "funeral-licker" by one and all.

Father was moaning that he lacked the seeds urgently needed for planting. Diravi was angry that Father should be so improvident. He never seemed to learn by experience; every year, it was the same. There was no seed for the first harvest; for the second, the water failed; for the third, there was too much of wind, and so on round the year. Neighbour Annamalai Pillai commiserated with him, but as it was getting late for the opening of his shop, he left.

Father called Diravi and bade him go to "Mother Hen" Arumugam and ask him whether he had any seeds to sell, failing which could give seedlings for Father's fields. The farmer Arumugam was invariably referred to by everyone as "Mother Hen" because he was a stay-at-home who refused to emerge unless there was great provocation or some urgent work.

Mother chose this moment to make her demands.

"We have received a letter from Pazhavadai that the first birthday ceremony of grandson is on Monday..."

"What do you need for that?" Father showed signs of getting angry, for he knew what was coming.

"We should make a gold chain or a girdle for the boy. And I do not have a good sari to wear if I have to go to Pazhavadai. All that I have is torn and old." Diravi had noticed Mother wearing saris that were patched in many places and pitied her, but he was not sure that this was the best moment to mention it to Father. Mother never did seem to know what to say to Father and when. She always seemed to choose the worst moment for everything.

Father began shouting as Diravi expected he would. "Every morning, I worry about what to do for the day's necessary expenses. You want new clothes and jewels made and bought...what else do you need? Do your father, mother, brothers, or sisters help me in anything? I bear the brunt of everything by myself with no help, no help at all!" Mother too said something in a loud voice, Unnamalai Aachi arrived to join in, pointing out what was fair and unfair in the whole thing. Finally, Mother broke down, and wailing loudly, she went into the kitchen. Diravi escaped from the place to go in search of "Mother Hen" Arumugam, thinking that anyhow mother would get her new sari and the girdle for the child, no matter whatever was said and however it was done.

His mission to "Mother Hen" Arumugam was a failure. There was some ceremony, which Arumugam had been discussing with his wife. Irritably, he turned to Diravi and said, "No." And when he went to Father and told him so, Father said sarcastically, "This boy is least useful to me. Whatever he does, does not bear fruit."

He left the house in a hurry after that; where to, no one knew.

Leaving Nagu Akka and Unnamalai Aachi at home the next Monday, everyone set off to celebrate the first birthday of Unnamalai Akka's son. Diravi wondered at the child's growth in a year. The chubby child was bright and active, taking two or three steps on his own, before falling down. When he laughed, two small teeth were visible. He minded all that was said, though he couldn't speak yet and danced to the words of his grandfather, moving his limbs and body appropriately.

The auspicious birthday ceremony was noisy and all the relatives assembled together again—the women talking, joking and singing together, moving about with the murmur of new silks—Mother too among them, and the men talking of the past and of things of general interest. The child was fondled by everybody and presents were heaped on him. He looked brave in new clothes and jewellery. He was named Iyappan and called thrice by that name which was a compromise between the name of his Paatta (Father's father) and God's name. The child was to be made to eat rice for the first time that day and his father sat holding him in his lap. On the leaf spread before them was served food of six tastes—sweet, sour, hot, bitter, half-bitter, and salty. The boy responded heartily to his father's fingers dipped in the respective dishes.

Then, all the guests sat down to a good feast. Later, while the men sat chewing betel, the talk turned to the possibility of there being the *kozhukattai*[1] festival that year, as the planets were in the conjunction necessary for it. The festival took place at the Odupparai temple only when the stars and planets were in a particular postion. It did not occur every year. It was the festival special to the Seven Towns' Chettiar community.

Diravi did not understand all the talk about it, for he had never seen one of the festivals, but had heard of its importance from the source of all his traditional knowledge—Unnamarai Aachi. As soon as he returned from Pazhavadai, he talked to her further about it and tried to learn about the festival and its merits.

"Odupparai serpent goddess, Nagarammai, is the family deity of the Seven Towns' Chettiars. Wherever a Chetti is, he will have to spend money and come to Odupparai and bake *kozhukkattai*."

"How do you bake *kozhukkattai*?" asked Diravi, not really knowing.

"Oh you crazy fellow…this is not the ordinary small *kozhukkattai* they usually make at home. Each *kozhukkattai* is made of half a measure of rice flour, a pound of powdered sugar, a coconut, cardamom, dried ginger, and fruits. No water should be added. Only the moisture of the fruits and sugar should hold the *kozhukkattai* together. Making it is an art; you will see for yourself in 78 months," Aachi informed him.

Diravi found there was only talk of the Odupparai festival; it was going to be a big event. From the Chitrai month onwards, all the houses in Eraniyal were busy with arrangements for the festival. Houses were newly whitewashed by those who could afford it; when they could not, the women cleaned their houses and walls with wet cloth, telling old tales: sometimes to new and, sometimes, to bored listeners.

The temple *kozhukkattai*s were the first lot to be fired for baking, by the priest. Thereafter, the private parties made ready to bake their *kozhukkattai*s. Father dug a deep trench in the open field and spread a layer of firewood in it. Then, a layer of *kozhukkattai* was arranged on it and, over it all, they spread more firewood. Next, the whole thing was fired. Slowly, the fire spread till the whole thing was burning yellow and evenly.

Some were ready to bake in the oven that was already fired and hot. Kuttalam too was busy over his *kozhukkattai*; so, he did not seek out his friend. The smoke was heavy and rose to the heavens. Eyes were smarting. Diravi was sleepy with all this activity and the crowd and the air, thick with smoke. He would rather have gone home, but there was no one there or even in the town. Everybody was here, at the festival.

In the pandal[2] erected at one end for the purpose, there was the telling of the tale of Nandan by Tarabhai. It was heard over the loudspeaker by those who stopped to listen to it. "Neelappillai is in her period; she could not come," said Ponamu Aachi sadly. Some were sleeping on the bare earth without even a towel under them. Some were talking of their past experiences and memories of the Odupparai festival.

Diravi was weary after the day's excitement and fell asleep with his head in Aachi's lap. He woke at midnight and looked up at the calm blue sky, full of stars…it seemed like a floor covered in flowers. A star left its cluster like a firework and brightly traced its way across the sky. He faintly heard some noises, but, without sorting them out, fell asleep again to wake up to someone calling him, "Diravi, Diravi." Mother was calling him. It was dawn. "The big cooking is on. Have your bath," said Mother.

The young sun was low in the east. The moon was pale and dull in the morning light. Thc stars that were visible looked like dull points fading out. In a short while, not one would be seen in the sky.

The smell of *kozhukkattai*s filled the air. Men and women who had already bathed were making ready the *padaiyal*[3] food. The river, Valli, flowed close by and all of them went to bathe in the clear, murmuring stream. When Diravi came back after his bath, he saw that Father and Brother-in-law had put the *kozhukkattai*s before the idols adorned with sandal-paste and multi-coloured flowers and clothes. There was a huge circle of citrus fruits encircling the two images. The decoration was said to be by a Thiruvanemanthapuram florist. The bells clanged. The camphor was waved in such a way that the devotee got a clear darshan of the god and goddess. This mass faith caused a strange ecstasy of devotion in Diravi.

Families which had come from far off began to return with their things in their carts. The festival was over. A few newcomers were abusing those who had been responsible for the early darshan—they were late. It would have developed into a big quarrel, but they compromised somehow.

The Eraniyal women cooked their *ponkal*[4] in long rows. But it was exactly at that moment that the news spread among all those present in the Odupparai temple. Ponamu Aachi's daughter, Neelappillai Aunt, and her son, Chidambaram, were not to be found in the house… Koonangani Paatta and Ponamu Aachi rushed back home. Father and others followed in a hurry.

The women could leave only after the *ponkal* was done and the noon worship over. It was after the noon puja that they left and arrived at Eraniyal to hear the whole thing; Chidambaram's teacher, Korami, also was missing. It was not long before everyone knew the tale and put two and two together. Everyone was whispering among themselves. "But a cow that has tasted hay will go to the hayrick." Some said that Neelapillai Aunt was already carrying Korami's child.

Diravi came home only late in the day. He waited for the evening puja also after the others of his house had left. But he could not stay there after the puja, for he was told that snakes would haunt the place where people had camped the night before.

Twenty-one

Koonangani Paatta's home looked like a house in mourning. "Nowadays, widows do not behave properly; they are not modest and restrained; they don't observe our customs. As soon as the husband dies, the widow casts about for another fellow." This was Unnamalai Aachi, who was old fashioned and had been a widow for many years.

She reminisced about losing her husband, without any passion—it was only a distant memory. "Dorai was only 5 or less when his father died. Everyone knew that he had a consumption problem, but since he was the right groom, I was married to him. Weddings were a great thing in those days; *my* wedding was. Everyone talked about it for days: the procession, the music concert..."

"He died. I was not even 20 yet; I was younger than Neelappillai. I wept and wept for days and retired into the darkest comer of the house to be by myself. Not one year or two, but for 10 years, I nursed my sorrow. Today, it is difficult to distinguish between one who is a widow and one who is not. It was only the care of the family and the responsibility of bringing up my son that sustained me. This is the age of Kali; it will get worse. What can anyone say?"

Aachi was voicing her dissatisfaction with the state of things after Neelappillai Aunt ran away with her lover. Diravi remembered another wife, Papathi, who had discarded her husband even while he lived. "They have searched for her everywhere. Where could she have disappeared to so completely in such a short while?" Mother expressed surprise.

"It must be easy to stay hidden. She'd been waiting for an opportunity to run away. It offered itself when all of us were at the festival. Who can say that they have not been planning for this for a long time?" Aachi rationalised.

Whatever the comments offered, what had happened could not be changed. Diravi was shocked at first, but the shock wore off in the course of a few days. He had seen how Korami and Neelappillai Aunt had behaved that day. No one was answerable to anyone else in that house—in a house which acknowledged no head, such events and worse were quite likely to occur.

Unnamalai Akka and Brother-in-law took their share of the *kozhukkattai*s and left for Pazhavadai. Diravi distributed some of it in the houses of those friends who had not come for the festival—mainly people from other communities. He liked the *kozhukkattai* very much. It smelled sweet and tasted quite nice. "It will keep like this for a year. It is Nagaramman's *prasadam*[1]," Aachi said and preserved what was left over, for later use.

Ponamu Aachi was shaken beyond recovery. She wailed loud and long, beat herself on the chest and mouth, thinking of her daughter and grandson and took to her bed. All the men of the house searched high and low for the missing persons, but could not find them. They blamed Ponamu for having been lax. Ananji Pillai Aachi was glad on the whole and tried to gossip about it all the time. The head-shaking old woman tried to console Ponamu Aachi when she became bedridden. "Every house has its scandal and its back door. Don't worry too much about it." Diravi was surprised at what the old woman had told Aachi. "Chetti families are stinking with scandals these days."

Koonangani Paatta was even more crushed; he was completely overwhelmed.

The SSLC results were announced. To everyone's enormous relief, Diravi had passed. That was great indeed.

Everybody was pleased. He was the first person in the family to pass the SSLC, On his parents instructions, he wrote to his Padmanabhapuram grandfather and to Uncle Pandaram Pillai, *in English*, the news of his having cleared the exam. Many who had started school with him had dropped out and were employed in shops or offices earning something by now. They had not even made it the final year. Only one fellow, Sivan Pillai, from the house on the main road, was preparing to go to college. He was strutting about proudly; he was considered a rich fellow, having inherited the property of a sister married to a rich family; her husband had been bitten by a mad dog and had died barking like one. Before he died, the father-in-law (Sivan Pillai's father), Velan Pillai, had made the rabid man write a will in the boy's favour, bequething all his property. He had since doubled the money by wise investments and trade. They had left the sister to roam the streets like a beggar, while they enjoyed the riches that were rightly her due. But Diravi did not know exactly how true the tales were.

As far as Diravi was concerned, there was no talk or thought of going to college. He could not afford it. The family was sliding financially; he had to do his share for its upliftment. His responsibilities were great and inescapable. But jobs were not easy to get. Draping his towel, neighbour Annamalai Pillai suggested, "He has passed the SSLC, but is not old enough to get a government job; it will take another year or two. Let him go to the basic training school for teachers at Neyyattinkarai and study. He can get a job as a teacher somewhere immediately. You do not need great recommendations for an appointment as a teacher."

Even though it would mean another period of waiting, Father was pleased with the idea. It was indeed a credit to be a teacher. Diravi joined the basic training school. Mother readied a food package for his lunch and he would set out early in the morning to the market, where he boarded a bus. It was usually dusk when he returned. He had little time to think of Nagu Akka, but the memory of her sorrow lurked in the background of his thoughts. Was she to spend her whole life like that? The question often troubled Diravi.

"Give these two *chakrams* for the Sastan[2] Koil blasting; let Sastan blast[3] our sorrows out of existence," said Aachi and gave him two *chakrams* which she had collected. Diravi knew that Aachi was thinking of Nagu. Aachi had plans for Nagu... Diravi was not sure, but he dared not question Aachi's expectations and hopes.

Vellachi, the fishwife, brought news of Sevantha Perumal's house for all the town to know. "The old lady has become skin and bones. It is the young lady who rules the house with an iron hand. There is no appeal beyond her word. She sends most of the household goods and groceries to her mother's house. The old lady dares not question her."

"By 'the old lady' Vellachi meant Papathi and by 'the young lady' she meant Sevantha Perumal's second wife, Vadivu. Papathi and her son were now reaping the results of their wrongdoing. It pleased Diravi, but did not profit Nagu in any way. Sevantha Perumal had charged Nagu Akka with not being a female. But it was more than two years since he had married Vadivu and there was no sign of a child yet. Did it not prove that it was Sevantha Perumal who lacked manhood?

Diravi wanted to prove to the town that his Nagu Akka was not what her husband had accused her of being. There was gossip about Sevantha Perumal's manly prowess. But would he be right in putting Nagu Akka in the public eye again, thought Diravi. He wanted to do it, but was afraid of the psychological burden he would be placing on himself and on his sister. Diravi was terribly confused.

Kuttalam was the subject of much talk in the town. His grandmother, who had had some control over him, had died. His father was a paralytic. The talk was that the boy had even fought with his father. Kuttalam was not welcome anywhere;

everybody tried to exclude him from their group. No one was sympathetic to him; no one helped him. It was said that he distilled and sold illicit liquor; they said he drank and visited prostitutes. These days, after he had begun to attend the teachers' training school, Diravi met Kuttalam rarely.

There were those who did not like his friendship with Kuttalam and even took it upon themselves as trustees of the community to advise him against it. But these same trustees had taken an unfriendly stance in the matter of Nagu Akka and Sevantha Perumal. Diravi held it against them and did not heed their advice at all. He did this to spite the elders of the community for the wrong they had done to Nagu Akka. Diravi thought that there were injustices and wrongdoings even in families that were apparently not rocked by scandals. Why were the elders ineffective in putting down these injustices in their community? Diravi was haunted by these thoughts.

One day, he heard that Sevantha Perumal Pillai was beaten severely by a drunken Kuttalam. He was returning from the market having closed his shop. Diravi wanted to meet Kuttalam and clarify a few doubts that had been troubling him. Kuttalam lived in a small house at the end of Puthan Street. While he was going towards Kuttalam's house, he reflected on Puthan Street, which, though known as "new", consisted mostly of old houses in bad repair. On the outer verandah of Sevantha Perumal's house, which was one of the better houses in the street, stood Vadivu, his wife; she was fair and well-preserved. She was well-dressed and wore heavy jewellery. She was a changing girl. Diravi thought that she smiled at him. He hurried away from the place with hatred in his heart. Some boys were playing games at the end of the street, which narrowed at this point. How many days had Diravi not played like this with boys of his age? There were batches of girls also playing games that were recognised as girls' games. Diravi prided himself on being an expert even in them. He heard some of the songs which accompanied these games and mused that they had been handed down from generation to generation—words which had none or little meaning. Did other lands have games and songs like these?

Everyone knew his own songs and games, nothing else, he thought.

Skin and bones, paralysed, Kuttalam's father lay in the deserted house. He was helpless and had no one to look after him. He did not recognise Diravi and could not speak. Their neighbour, a woman, said that Kuttalam would come home only at night. Recognising Diravi with difficulty, she began to talk of Nagu Akka's misfortune. He escaped from her hurriedly, and passed the youngsters playing blindman's buff. How many children there were in this crowded place! All of them certainly did not live here; it would be too crowded.

He met Kuttalam just opposite the paan shop. "I have been to your house," Diravi informed him.

"To my house?" asked Kuttalam, surprised.

"You should not leave your father alone and helpless like this."

"But I had to go to the doctor…I have to earn my living. There is no one to help. What can I do?"

They went to the river, the bed of which was half dry.

"Diravi…I hate this place. I would like to go somewhere else and live peacefully."

For a while, both of them were silent. Then Kuttalam said, "I am waiting here only to light my father's pyre; then I can leave without looking back. What have I here to hold me back? I did not like my father when he was able and moving about; but now, as he lies dying, I realise how dear to me he is."

Diravi washed his face in the river and talked about what he had come to say to Kuttalam. "I was told that you beat the fellow."

Kuttalam did not immediately remember whom he had beaten. For him, it was one among many such incidents. "Brother-in-law..." Diravi reminded him.

Kuttalam was enraged. "You call him 'Brother-in-law' after all that has happened? ... I saw the fellow coming. West Street Thanu Pillai was with me. Even the way he walked irritated me. I said that there were a few maharajas here who walked with stiff limbs anticipating their next girl.

Thanu Pillai was drunk and he said, "Chettis don't do anything without profit to themselves." Sevantha Perumal got angry. "Eh, fool. Whom did you call Chetti without respect." I told him that he was being referred to as the fellow who is neither male, nor female. Immediately, he sprang at me, holding up the huge key of his shop. I got hold of the key, threw it at him, and gave him a few blows that must have made his ears ring..." Kuttalam laughed with delight at the memory of the fight.

Diravi knew the cause of Kuttalam's hatred for that fellow. He too would have liked to have taught Sevantha Perumal a lesson, if not in a physical sense, at least, through words. "But don't do anything like this any more, Kuttalam. It will lead to trouble for us," pleaded Diravi. Kuttalam did not reply to that, but when Diravi was leaving, he asked him the usual question, "How is Nagu?"

Two days later, when Diravi was setting out to school, Father called him and said, "It is better for you to not be friendly with that fellow Kuttalam." Diravi did not reply. "Do you know what people are saying in town—that you asked Kuttalam to beat Sevantha Perumal..."

Diravi was surprised. He disliked being silent in the face of this slur to his self-respect, "If I want to beat anyone, I shall not ask another to do it. I shall do so myself," he said and walked away, his face red and excited. During school hours, he thought about what his father had told him. Did Nagu Akka also think that he had had her husband beaten by his friend?

It was dusk when he came back home from school. Aachi was telling Salam, "Hold this iron key in your hand. It will keep the ghosts from harming you." Salam was standing in a corner away from people. Nagu Akka saw Diravi and said that Salam had matured. "When?" asked Diravi wondering. And was told "just now."

Mother added, "At noon, the oil caught fire when I was frying papads. 'The household fire laughs when a girl matures' is the proverb. I knew that Salam would mature before the end of the day." She was proud of her powers of prognostication. "Today is Rohini[4]: it is a good star," Aachi pontificated.

Diravi looked at Salam. Poor girl—she was quite young to take on the responsibilities of a woman. She was afraid of the hubbub. She was close to tears and Diravi's reflection's were tinged with sorrow. Nagu Akka was caught in a mess. May God prevent something like that happening to Salam, the innocent child that she was.

He wanted to see Salam laugh amidst her worries. "You have become a big woman!" he said.

Salam was always ready to laugh. Anything would set her off—somebody sneezing, something moving in the breeze, or someone asking where she had been. Mother and Aachi would tell her that a girl should not laugh so much; it was not good for her. Diravi's words were enough to set her laughing shyly, her head down, but proud at having become a woman.

Mother mixed some sandal paste, kumkum, and saffron, and gave it to Salam to drink. She was told that she could eat only after she'd bathed. The mixture was not pleasant and she took it as she would take medicine, making all sorts of faces...

Father arrived. Koonangani Paatta and all his household, except Ponamu Aachi who was bedridden, came visiting. Andi Pillai Uncle was sent to Pazhavadai by bus to bring

Unnamalai Akka and her husband. Now, buses were plying between the two places—the journey was more pleasant and speedier than by cart. Ammalu, the aunt, had to arrive before Salam could be bathed. "Ammalu won't come quite so easily." But her presence was essential.

Picha Pillai Uncle was sent to Kolachel to explain the necessity to Ammalu Aunt and prevail upon her to come. Aunt Thayi and neighbour Annamalai Pillai's wife went from house to house in town inviting people to attend the ceremony. Diravi was sent to the market to get plantains, betel leaves, nuts, and sugar. When he came back, the house was full of people. Salam sat where she had been. A number of women were sitting round her, cracking jokes.

The piper arrived and piped away noisily. Unnamalai Akka and her husband had also arrived. It was midnight when everything was ready. The women sang *koluvai*. The pedestal light was lit. Salam brushed her teeth. She was asked to pour coconut milk on her head and was bathed in cold water. She was asked to rub turmeric[5] paste which was ready, on her face. Aunt Ammalu bathed her ritually and ceremoniously. She was asked to wear a new dress. They distributed fruits and sugar to all present; even rice cooked in milk was distributed.

Salam, who had had nothing to eat all day, was hungry. She was not allowed to eat till everyone had left. By that time, Salam was so sleepy that she forgot her hunger and did not get to eat at all.

Twenty-two

The house was full of people coming and going and gossiping. They came to enquire after Salam, who had matured. Till the ceremony was over, Salam had to remain in her corner; she could not go where she pleased in the house.

Father managed to get some money. Of course, money was scarce, but these ceremonies had to be observed properly. They distributed fruits and sweets to all the houses in town. Visalam was given eggs, sesame oil, black-gram rice, sweets and other things, by turns. She might be the third girl, but all the ceremonies due to her had to be done. Aachi would not allow any relaxation of the observances, however difficult the situation was. When Diravi's other sisters, matured these ceremonies must have been celebrated. Why, even when his mother and Aachi matured long ago, all these ceremonies had been observed—perhaps, with more gusto and glory than now. What was the meaning of all these ceremonies, Diravi wondered. He supposed they had a meaning.

The final ceremony was to be observed on the 14th day, which was considered auspicious. It was as far as Diravi could see, a mock wedding between Salam and Aunt Ammalu; it was the aunt's right to play the part of the groom for the occasion. There was also a Brahmin murmuring mantras at this wedding. All the ceremonies he remembered from Nagu Akka's wedding were carried out, but on a smaller scale. It was like a rehearsal of Salam's wedding. All the relatives were there—all those Diravi could remember, and some, he did not, from Nagu's wedding.

Neelappillai Aunt's affairs were freely talked about. Everybody said that widows today were not what they used to be in the old days, and that Chetti families were going from bad to worse without any financial improvement. Simpleton that he was, Mother's father was mixing up old stories and narrating two stories as one. Talk of Nagu Akka continued in a low pitch.

It was a familiar story by now.

It transpired that Aachi had made Father spend quite a bit of money in the ceremonies attending Salam's attainment of puberty. But it was clear that Kuzhalamangai had matured and no ceremonies had been undertaken, though it was four months since she had matured. This became known when Ammalu came, leaving her daughter with her mother. She was called miserly, more miserly than her husband; even though they were rich, they had not spent a single *chakram* on the ceremonies that marked puberty. Even Mother's father, who talked so loftily about other things, was helpless when it came to the miserliness of his son. "It is his wealth. Who are we to ask him to spend it?" he would say.

Diravi's examinations were on. He was reading late at night and was becoming aware that except Aachi, the old woman, and the young Salam, no one in the house slept long or peacefully. Father would murmur, "Nagaraja[1]! Father! My Lord," and turn in his bed quite often. Mother and Nagu also did not sleep well at all. Salam was always a sleepy head. Aachi had a great burden of worries, but she delegated her burdens to God and fate and to a traditional wisdom that allowed her to sleep in peace. Nothing is in our hands. Everything will happen according to fate. No one can prevent what has to happen. The gardener who plants the trees will not forget to water them," she would often say, demonstrating complete faith in the unknown.

Diravi was subject to more and more wounds as time passed. In the midst of studying, he would stop, overwhelmed by the sorrows that he saw around him. Aachi belonged to a generation before his father's. Aachi's generation, with a few exceptions, was able to place all their responsibilities at God's feet and get away with it. Father and Mother were not able to do it so successfully. They felt responsible, but helpless.

They could only curse their helplessness. But Diravi was young, and belonged to the modern generation. He felt responsible for his sister's fate; he felt he had to do something to alter it. But how? By doing what? He was not yet sure.

Mechanically, he studied for his exams and wrote them. His mind was full of thoughts of revenge and kindred things. He wrote his last exam and when he returned home after taking leave of his friends, it was two hours past lighting time. He was feeling extremely hungry. He hurried home, noticing that a crowd had gathered in Koonangani Paatta's house.

Someone was shouting. He went home, washed, changed, and sat down to eat what was available. Mother served *aviyal*, potato curry, rice, and then, the vegetable sambhar. When he began to eat, she said, "There was a big quarrel in Thayi's house. Ananji Pillai has taken Thayi and the boy to her house." Diravi was not surprised; he had expected that some such thing would happen.

Mother then added, "Kolappa Uncle and his accountant in the shop, Andaruma Pillai, had a quarrel, some two months ago, about the accountant's salary. As, owner of the shop, Uncle dismissed his accountant. Andaruma Pillai to wreak vengeance gave information to the sales tax authorities about a number of transactions on which uncle had not paid tax. The sales tax officers came in a jeep and when business was roaring, sealed it, and took away all the account books. But Uncle's crime was that there were no bills to account for the money in the cash box. They also found out that there were quite a number of things in stock, which were not accounted for. They even searched his house and it is said that he removed a number of secret account books all on the information given by Andaruma Pillai who had been denied a little more as salary.

The case was pending and would be settled in due course. Uncle was fined an amount he could not raise easily. There was no possibility of relief on appeal, for Uncle was caught with the goods as it were. The way they were spending money was well known in town; Thayi was a spendthrift; her husband had no control over her. She lost more things than people were able to buy in a lifetime—especially jewels and silk saris. More food was wasted in her house than anywhere else in town. The henpecked fellow, your uncle, let his wife spend as she liked; even when his mother tried to correct her, she fell foul of her son who encouraged his wife. Kolappa Uncle himself had spent a lot of money on the singer Kokila, who was young and beautiful. The whole town of Eraniyal knew the story. Inspite of all this, his business was good so long as Anadaruma Pillai was running it. After his accountant left, Uncle was anyhow getting ready to sell his shop, convert everything into cash, go to Tiruvancode and live modestly with whatever he had. But as soon as he made it known, Aunt began quarrelling with him, saying that she did not want to go to that small village. There was nothing else that Uncle could do under the circumstances. And this sales tax case was making a criminal of him. If he did not pay the fine, he would have to go to jail and count bars. He was unable to heed his wife, who was getting more and more angry with him.

Diravi ate his buttermilk and rice, and washed his hands and saw Aachi muttering, with great dissatisfaction, "What is wrong with Tiruvancode? It is a good, small place where you can live comfortably. The well water there is very sweet. There is a temple, there are men and women living there. All round are famous temples at a comfortable distance. And the people are better, much better, and less inclined to gossip and quarrel, than people in this hopeless place called Eraniyal." Aachi's voice was hoarse, suggesting that she had been shouting all day. She was panting from her exertions. She was always against Thayi for her obstinacy and her ways. She continued, "Even if she does not like a place, wherever her husband goes, she has to follow. That is a wife's duty. She has lived like a queen here. What did he deprive her of that she should quarrel like this with him? She says, "You go; I won't come' and dances a bhangra[2] in the street."

From what he heard, Diravi could guess what had happened. Uncle was ready to leave, but Aunt did not want to go and would not allow him to take their son either. The mother-in-law took her son's side, albeit he did not treat her well and, for that, was roundly abused. The whole street had collected and tried to advise the woman. Koonangani Paatta was away in the fields. Ananji Pillai and her son, Andi Pillai, went and made matters worse.

"I brought up my daughter like a pet parrot and not for anyone to kill her like this," began Ananji Pillai, without rhyme or reason. Andi Pillai shouted, "I will not allow anyone to take my sister against her wishes." Between them, they persuaded Thayi Aunt to go with them to the house of her father, Koonangani Paatta.

Unnamalai Aachi told Diravi, "I pleaded with Ananji Pillai that what she was doing was wrong. I asked them not to be obstinate about this. The girl has to be with her husband. You know the fate of our Nagu. We were not responsible for it, but for this, you will be responsible. If he marries someone else, what will be the fate of your daughter? I shouted at her, till I was hoarse. But she would not listen. 'He will come of his own accord. Where will he go? Go home, Aunt. I don't need your advice,' said Thayi. What folly, what bravado, what unwomanly behaviour!" Exclaimed Aachi, surprised out of her normalcy.

Kolappa Uncle left that very day with his mother for Tiruvancode, leaving the house and all the things he had accumulated in the shop and the house, to pay for the fine.

Koonangani Paata, on coming back from the fields at night, heard the news and shouted at every one in the house. But nobody minded him. They had stopped listening to him a long time ago. There was no historical evidence that he had ever been listened to in his house. Poor man.

Twenty-three

The exam results were announced. Diravi had passed once more. But even then, getting a job was not so easy. If he could not get a job in a government school, he thought he would get one in a private school. But unless he was willing to give a bribe of a thousand rupees, no jobs were to be had. He could not imagine remaining idle. But where was he to get a thousand rupees? At last, his house was shown as collateral and a thousand rupees borrowed from community trustee Velu Pillai. If a month's interest was overdue, they were to vacate the house and hand it over to Velu Pillai. Diravi joined a private school and discovered that he had signed for one amount and received something less than that. Even that he was not able to get every month; once in three or four months, he might, if he was lucky, be paid.

In the process, Father lost all his illusions about the dignity of the teaching profession. Aachi was also disappointed, "You studied, you passed, you got a job; yet how mean and small minded the world is," she said.

As soon as Salam matured, her schooling ceased. Diravi tried to make them consent to her going to school, but the older women in the house were sure that the dark corner, which had been theirs when they were virgins, should be Salam's also.

It was a middle school which Diravi had joined. There were classes up to the 8th grade. He found that teaching came easily to him. But he was worried about his two sisters. One, Nagu, married and yet living with them, and the other, Salam, unmarried and destined to a dark corner in the house for years to come. They were problems ever present in his mind.

One morning, there was a hubbub in front of Koonangani Paatta's house. Diravi woke up early in the morning to voices raised in anger. Kolappa Uncle was shouting into the house, "Eh, Thayi. If that boy is mine and not someone else's then come with me and bring my son. If you don't come, I will take my son away. You hear me?"

The residents of the street were assembling to watch and to arrive at some sort of compromise and to suggest all sorts of things. Uncle's eyes were red with anger. But Ananji Pillai Aachi replied to him as loudly, "She is not coming with you. Nor is the child, my grandson. You go. Don't make a din here early in the morning, you drunkard."

Thayi Aunt also said something, but Diravi did not know what. A street quarrel is always easy on the eye. Men and women watched with interest and assembled, each suggesting a different thing, in the name of fairness and justice. Diravi also went and tried to pacify Uncle and send him home. But in the course of time it, became a daily occurrence. Sometimes, Uncle would jump into the house and, obstinately, pull the boy out while Aunt set up a roar, "He is trying to kill my child!" Father and Diravi and others would join in retrieving the child and sending Uncle away.

If anyone had told Diravi that very quickly, a respectable family would reach such depths unthought of before, he would not have believed it. But it was happening before his eyes. Kolappa Uncle had sunk much lower than anyone he had known, in record time. This was because of his wife whom he loved well, but unwisely. If he left his wife alone for a few days, she would voluntarily have gone to him with the child. Things were not well for her or for anybody in her mother's house. But he forced the issue and got a bad name for himself. Diravi was angry with Ananji Pillai Aachi and Thayi Aunt.

What fools they were.

Ponamu Aachi was still bedridden. Neelappillai Aunt had disappeared once and for all. No one discovered her whereabouts. Ponamu never recovered from that sorrow of hers. It was rumoured that once she wept and told Koonangani Paatta, "If only I had had the wisdom to listen to you when young, our house would not have suffered thus …but I have one desire to see Iya Pillai married. He is way past the normal age of marriage; if allowed to go on like this, he will destroy himself." She was not dying, but very close to it; she was quite helpless. It was difficult to make Iya Pillai consent to marriage. It was rumoured that he had a keep in some Pandarathi's house in eastern Mandapam. But bowing to the dying wish of his mother, he agreed.

Iya Pillai's reputation was so bad that no one who knew of him would come forward to give him his daughter in marriage. He was also past the marriageable age. In Kallukkatti, there was the granddaughter of a man called the big-lathi Pothi; she was left with no help, but her father's mother. She was called Velammai. She was also quite old, nearly a spinster. They were living in extreme poverty with hardly anything to eat or wear and not even oil to use before a bath. She was a virgin. The old woman agreed and the marriage was celebrated.

Aachi explained to Diravi how the bride's grandfather came to be called the Big-lathi Pothi. "This fellow would go to every house where someone had died and leave his big stick and shoes in a corner, so that everyone who came to condole with the family thought that the fellow was somewhere there, having arrived dutifully long before they themselves had. After the corpse was carried away from the house, he would ask someone to retrieve his stick and shoes. This was a secret for a long time, but everyone came to know of it eventually. And when he himself died, for death comes to everyone, the whole town left their sticks and their shoes in his house, and did not personally attend the funeral, so that he had a veritable forest of sticks and shoes as his mourners. Everyone thereafter called him the big-Lathi Pothi in honour of the joke." Whatever it was, the Big-lathi Pothi's granddaughter was now Diravi's Aunt.

Ponamu Aachi did not recover, at the marriage or afterwards. She had diabetes and Velammai could be seen making gooseberry extract for her. Shortly after her son's marriage, Ponamu Aachi developed an abscess in her back and more painful than the abscess, was the way Ananji Pillai Aachi and her son, Andi Pillai, talked to her. Iya Pillai Uncle continued as usual; his marriage did not work any change in him in any way. If he came home at night, it was a miracle. Poor Velammai shed many tears; had she remained unmarried, she had been better off. Picha Pillai Uncle was different; he dutifully attended to his mother and her needs. Koonangani Paatta tried to cure Ponamu Aachi with a lot of medicines; no one else cared for her very much. But one night, she died suddenly, not recovering consciousness to suffer anymore.

The funeral expenses were a matter of loud debate in the house; even the essentials were forbidden by Ananji Pillai Aachi and her son, Andi Pillai. The other side was not less ably represented by Iya Pillai and Picha Pillai. Koonangani Paatta said nothing…they each wanted to partition all the properties even while Ponamu Aachi's corpse lay in the house. Diravi, his father, and Unnamalai Aachi tried to reason with them, but to no purpose. "They call themselves wife and son and relatives Father, Unnamalai Aachi and Diravi" thought Diravi bitterly. "Why does a little money make demons of men and women? Humans are not human when they are under the influence of money."

The quarrel continued for a long time, each side asserting what it wanted. Only, nobody wanted the house; so, long went the *kurukshetram*[1] of the family. The matter was referred to the court. Quarrels and the case continued for a long while. Ponamu Aachi was dead; otherwise Father, Unnamalai Aachi and Diravi she too would have joined the melee to make life miserable for Koonangani Paatta. The partition took place according to the orders of the court. But Paatta had mentioned in court that a share was due to Ammachi, so that the least quarrelsome of the women around him would get her share in spite of the objections of all his sons. The result was that even after the partition every one of his legitimate sons was angry and declared vengeance on Koonangani Paatta.

After the partition, having got all they could get, Iya Pillai Uncle took his wife and younger brother Picha Pillai and went to Trivandrum saying that he was setting up a shop there. With them went Ponamu Aachi' svessels and bed and other miscellaneous things.

In the house were left Ananji Pillai Aachi, her daughter, Thayi Aunt, her son, and Andi Pillai Uncle along with Paatta. Kolappa Pillai Uncle often came and, standing outside in the street would raise his voice for his son. Everyone found fault with Andi Pillai for keeping Thayi, his sister, with him. They advised him to send her away with her husband. But Andi Pillai proudly declared that he would look after her. People were waiting for a time when he would bring a wife home and set the two women quarrelling. Thayi Aunt, ever a lover of loud and costly things and of going to the cinema, had not been affected by anything that had happened. Ananji Pillai Aachi also loved to wear silks. As for Andi

Pillai, he spent a lot on his terylene shirts, cigarettes and friends.

But Koonangani Paatta was growing visibly weaker and bowed. He was impatient and irritable. After his SSLC, Andi Pillai went to Nagercoil, completed a course for electricians, and got a job in a mill there. Ananji Pillai Aachi and her daughter were preparing to go with him, leaving Paatta behind to shift for himself. Father, Unnamalai Aachi, and Diravi tried to argue with them that it was wrong to leave the old man to himself like an orphan. Unnamalai Aachi was especially loud and insistent.

But Ananji Pillai Aachi was remorseless. "Ponamu Aachi died in bed. Her sons left their old man destitute and went away to enjoy themselves. Why should we, who owe him nothing more, remain here taking care of him in his old age, listening to his ravings, doing his bidding and medicating him? Why should we? I don't know; tell me."

When Diravi talked to Andi Pillai, he found that Thayi Aunt did not relish it. She shouted, "If anyone lives well, it will not be liked by others in this place. Brother has got a good job and goes to Nagercoil. We go to attend to his needs…a thousand persons stand in our way."

But Koonangani Paatta was unruffled. He said, "No one need remain here to take care of me or to give me medicine. All of you may go. But leave me in peace. That is all I want." He was very bitter, but did not prevent them by word or deed.

All of them left for Nagercoil town, where they could lead a better life, buy new clothes and see new films. As for money, the tenant would send them their share every year. Diravi, Father, Aachi, all of them tried to persuade Koonangani Paatta to come to their house for his meals, so that he would not have to cook himself. *But* he refused. Even when Unnamalai Aachi broke down and wept, he refused to listen. He said, "It is only for a short while; I will not leave this house where I have lived for such a long time. Nobody need worry about me."

Sometimes, Mother or Aachi would send him something that they had prepared. But he refused even that. Once he shouted at Diravi saying he did not want their help at all. The old man was in a passion of bitterness. Once Krishnan Kutty and Ammachi came to persuade him to accept their help, but he refused even that. In the house in which he had lived with so many persons, he delighted in his solitude. He was tired of men and women and their ways. The tenant brought him his share of rice as ordered by the court; he would sell what rice was not needed and buy the other things like salt, oil, etc., with the money, and he was content. He did not need anything more. Sometimes, when Diravi went to his house just to see him and talk to him, he would find him cooking or powdering something for cooking and be moved to tears. "At this age, why should you toil like this for your food?" Diravi would ask him. The old man would reply, "He who has eaten salt sometime or the other has to drink water; he cannot escape." He had some books in the house; pages of many of which were missing. His eyes watering, he would read aloud from these books to himself—it was the

Malulblulrata or *Tiruvilayadal* or *Garuda Puranam*, which one read only on funeral days in the house.

Unnamalai Aachi said to him one day, sobbing, "You had two wives, not one. Three grown boys; two girls, who have children of their own. Yet, not a dog comes near you to ask you how you are."

Paatta hesitated, as if in a trance for a while before replying, and then said, 'We have already enjoyed the affection we feel is due from our children and from our parents; there is nothing more to expect. We returned the love we enjoyed from our parents to our children. The account is balanced with that. They will show the affection we showed them to their children. We cannot expect anything from them; it is wrong to expect anything. I am not disappointed; if my father had expected affection from me, how disappointed he must have been."

Diravi, who was listening, was strangely affected by these words. He went out before they noticed the tears in his eyes.

Twenty-four

On Vijayadasami[1] day, Unnamalai Aakka's son's ear lobes were to be pierced. Brother-in-law had sent a letter. Father was busy in the fields and could not go; so, Diravi and his mother went to Pazhavadai.

Before the picture of Saraswathi, goddess of learning and the arts, who sat holding a veena, Brother-in-law sat with his son playing in his lap. But when his first ear lobe was pierced, the boy set up a wail that was really loud for a three-year-old. His other lobe was pierced even while he was weeping and the earrings were put in. The women's auspicious songs drowned his wailing. Diravi could not recollect it, but felt that he too must have wept when his ears were pierced like this by the goldsmith. And must have later been proud of his earrings as now his nephew was. Uncle Iyan Pillai, the grandfather, was quite happy. The boy himself looked somewhat altered now, with his earrings. Everyone present received sweetened rice.

When Diravi returned to Eraniyal, Aachi handed over a letter addressed to him. It was an appointment order from the Karingal Government School. Diravi was pleased; it was a worthwhile change from private school service. Karingal was some miles on the road from Eraniyal to Kuzhithurai, but the bus service to Karingal was fairly regular. And the town itself was a big and busy one.

He had become an experienced teacher and loved teaching. Though the Karingal school was a High School, Diravi had to take classes only up to the 8th class. He arranged for some tuitions also, as there were some old debts to be cleared.

One day Diravi was sitting, lost in his endless, sorrowful thoughts in a dark comer of the staffroom when he heard someone ask him, "What is it Diravi? I have asked you half a dozen times…you always seem to be unhappy."

It was teacher Moses who stood beside him. Moses was one of the most loved men in the school; everyone had a special regard for him. He was quite bald with a few strands of white hair. He had a broad forehead. He wore glasses, from behind which his eyes laughed brightly. A prominent nose and beneath it a Hitlerian moustache. He wore a mull dhoti and a bush shirt. He was all of 6.6 ft tall. Moses had been asking him this question for quite some time. "Nothing really," was Diravi's usual reply.

Moses drew up a chair and sat in it. He stretched his legs on another chair and began to chew betel leaf as was his habit. There were only two or three other teachers in the large staff-room and they were gossiping.

"No, you are concealing something, Diraviam. You are only 20 years old …you should be happy at this age and in your circumstances. But you seem to be nursing some secret sorrow."

Diravi could not tell him anything. What was he to tell him?

Moses was a senior teacher in the school. He was nearly 50 years old. In a couple of years, he would become the Headmaster. He was usually called MAMA, because he had a double MA degree. He had a third division master's degree in literature; so he took maths and passed his second MA again in the third class. Not because he did not do well in his exam but because he was in the national movement and his teachers disqualified him, loyal British citizens that they were. He did not want to study for a third MA; so, he became a school teacher. His wife was a doctor in the Neyyor Hospital. He was well off now—both husband and wife were earning …but he was a modest, unassuming man. People always said, "Look at Moses. He has something to be proud of. But there is no pride in his make up. He is one in a thousand, an exception in these times." This was the tribute that even the school peon paid to Moses, while he borrowed snuff from him liberally.

With his fellow teachers as well as his superiors, Moses had the reputation of generally being a reliable man. He was frank and affectionate. Such a highly respected man was asking him something and Diravi did not want to lie to him. The bell rang and Moses said, "I have to take English for the tenth. We shall talk about it again," and left.

Leaving school that evening, he was caught by Moses again. "When I was your age, Diraviam, do you know how adventurous I was," he laughed, his laughter indicative of a thousand interesting stories. When he asked him again what his burden was, Diravi was embarrassed. What was he to say? Did he himself know what his burden was? He tried to examine himself. Nagu Akka's face was the first thing he remembered. And then quite a number of things. He had known hundreds of persons. With some, he had had happy moments. But he could think only of the sorrowful thing that had happened to him. Was he a weak person born to self-pity? Diravi wondered.

He had come across a number of problems and situations of his own, and others'. He had examined them deeply yet he was oppressed by the tragic, pitiable things he had experienced in his life. Why? He had mown a number of worthwhile persons—Koonangani Paatta, Ammachi Ammukkutti, Kuttalam, Kannu Pillai, Kolappa uncle, Neelappillai aunt, and Padmariabhapuram grandfather, but despite all these, he always remembered his sister Nagu and her pitiable countenance. He was unable to shake off that burden.

It was not a market day. So there was no crowd at the bus stand. When they had to wait sometime for the bus, Moses questioned him again. For the first time in his life Diravi spoke of his sister's plight to a third party.

"What was the reason for the break up?" asked Moses. Then Diravi was beset by doubts as to whether he had been right in telling Moses the story.

"To tell you the truth I myself am not able to say for certain," he confessed. He remembered the innuendoes of Papathi and Sevantha Perumal that Nagu Akka was not a woman. He said, "They said that she was not a woman. That is what I remember," and then he fell silent, afraid of having said too much.

Moses understood his reluctance to speak about it and respected it. They waited silently for the bus which had not yet come.

"You think it is not a fact, don't you?" Moses asked.

"Yes," nodded Diravi.

"Then why did you not Institute proceedings against him?"

"Father did not want to drag a private affair into the open court. I was not old enough at that time. But even now Father would not consent to go to court."

Moses went to a neighbouring shop, bought a cigarette, lit it at the smouldering string that hung in the shop and came back, by which time the bus had arrived. He drew a puff on the cigarette threw it away and got into the bus.

"What do you think was the real reason for their driving your sister out?"

Diravi thought about it and did not know what to say.

Moses also was deep in thought. Then he said, "Considering your sister as mine I shall tell you one thing I can think of—don't misunderstand me."

Diravi looked at him and saw the sympathy on his face. He had faith in Moses. The bus was nearing the place where Diravi had to get down. So, Moses said hurriedly, "You do something: you can't allow things to go on like this. You know my wife is a doctor in Neyyor hospital. Nobody need know anything of what you do. Take your sister one Sunday morning to my wife…no, not in the morning…she will be at Church. Take your sister sometime in the evening. Even your sister need not know for what purpose you are taking her, nor anyone else in the town. I shall tell Rosammai, my wife. Let her examine her, and then, we shall see what has to be done." The bus stopped. Diravi did not know what to say in reply. "Think about it. Tell me later."

Diravi got off and the bus drove away. He was thinking of Moses' suggestion, but it was not easily done. Nagu Akka had not come out of the house all these years. This was something to do, tangible, but was it practicable? How was he to manage it without anyone in the street or house knowing about it?

Someone called out to horn twice. It was Kuttalam. He waited for him and they walked on together. Though Kuttalam looked tired, his moustaches were majestic. "I am opening a small shop in the market," he said.

"What shop?" Diravi asked.

"Guess."

When Diravi could not guess, Kuttalam said, "Eraniyal lace cloth is famous. I shall open a shop for the sale of lace cloth."

He took him through of a short cut, by which they had to pass Lakshmi Atha's hut. When Diravi remarked on it, Kuttalam said, "They have gone away to the Leprosy Centre at Nooranadu. She sold her buffaloes and cows and gave him the money to go to hospital when he did not want to ask his son."

The wife and son who were enjoying the man's property were unwilling to help him, and he was unwilling to ask them a favour, but someone who was a keep and had no legal status as wife had sold all she had to admit him in the hospital. Human relationships were truly wonderful and surprising, thought Diravi.

"How is your father?" he asked Kuttalam.

"I had almost given him up as dead, but he has slowly recovered. Now only his left leg is paralysed; otherwise, he is all right."

This was good news indeed. "I have to run home from time to time to prepare his medicine and to feed him. You know the help our neighbours can give us; it is practically non-existent. Only trouble. But when I open a shop, it is going to be more difficult."

Diravi knew that it was true. If Kuttalam had someone in the house to help him…he was at least seven or eight years older than Diravi was. If he married and brought a wife to the house to help...

"Why don't you marry?"

Diravi did not know whether he was wrong to have made such a suggestion directly to his friend. But Kuttalam made no reply. He did not seem to resent the question either. He just laughed, indicative of a reply he might have made. Then he asked, "Do you and your family still believe that Sevantha Perumal will relent and take Nagu back?"

Diravi was worried about whether it was an indirect reply to his question. Who could measure a man's mind? Was Kuttalam thinking of anything in particular?

Diravi did not say anything.

"My marriage, if it occurs, will not help me much. It might help my father a little. Nothing more. But I want to do one thing for certain," said Kuttalam. He seemed to have difficulty in expressing what he wanted to say. But he added, "In one sense what Sevantha Perumal did to your sister was the ultimate insult insult to womanhood. But when he married Vadivu after discarding your sister, what was he hoping to prove? Vadivu comes of a childbearing family. Sevantha Perumal has had no children... Now, Vadivu knows her husband's weakness. Vadivu is a sensible woman..."

"But Kuttalam, how do you know all these things?"

"To get your way, you have to cultivate even a donkey, says the proverb. Vadivu herself told me," said Kuttalam triumphantly. "But don't ask me anything more about this just now. Just believe that what I say is right. I hated him for what he did to Nagammai and I have always thought kindly of your sister. You can believe me on that."

Kuttalam had said many things indirectly to Diravi. But if he wanted to wreak vengeance on Sevantha Perumal, he was willing to go to any extent. Diravi had gained some peace of mind in talking to Moses. But after his talk with Kuttalam, he lost what little peace of mind he had gained.

Grandfather Subbu Pillai was famous for his revolutionary activities in the community, including the performance of a widow remarriage of his own sister 40 years ago. What Kuttalam planned was marrying a girl whose husband had cast her aside. While the world is allergic to secret relationships of all kinds, it condemns open defiance of customs and habits. "But it is these persons," Diravi thought, "who sanctioned and accepted Sevantha Perumal's second marriage after he had put aside his first wife."

Would anyone in his house consent to such a second marriage for Nagu? Would Nagu Akka herself accept it and be happy with it? What could he do in this matter, thought Diravi.

It was Sevantha Perumal who had created the problem in the first instance. He was responsible for whatever consequences it would now lead to. Diravi felt that he could not keep quiet under this insult as the older generation could and had. It was no use thinking revolutionary thoughts. One should act like a revolutionary. He had to wage a sacred war, which would call for all his skill and strength.

Twenty-five

When Diravi arrived home, many items of news were waiting for him.

Father was not present; Aachi and Mother told him what had happened.

Padmanabhapuram Subbu Pillai Grandfather, Grandmother, Uncle Pandaram Pillai—all three of them had come earlier that evening, seeking Diravi's horoscope for Kuzhalamangai Uncle's daughter. If the horoscopes agreed, they could talk further of marriage.

Father had said in a word, "Not just yet. One of my daughters has been set aside by her husband. Another has matured, and is awaiting marriage. Diravi is only 20 years old. We'll wait a few years."

All the visitors got angry. Grandfather's protest was loud. "What is wrong with Kuzhalamangai? Is she not rich? Is she not educated? Is she not good looking? Actually, Pandaram was not very favourably inclined to this wedding. But I thought that it would unite our families more closely. You should not kick the treasure that comes seeking you. Pandaram earns so much—you don't know what he earns per day!"

Father disliked the way his father-in-law shouted at him. Even in these, his most difficult days, he had never turned to his father-in-law and his rich brother-in-law for any help. They could have come forward to help him of their own accord; they had never done so. Father would never sacrifice his self-respect for momentary gain.

When they were young, the family used to think of Diravi and Kuzhali as a possible pair, an "item". But as Pandaram Uncle grew richer, all that was forgotten. Now that Diravi had passed his exams and was employed in a government school, they renewed their notion of him as a possible son-in-law. Why should grandfather insist that his rich granddaughter marry his poor grandson? Father had never been in love with money…he had never believed that money could buy everything in life.

The outcome was that Father refused to hand over Diravi's horoscope. They had quarrelled with Father and had left breathing vengeance. So far they had been relatives at least in name; hereafter they wouldn't even be that.

Diravi understood his Father's stand. He was sorry that Father had not been more curt with them than he had been. But the neighbours knew of the rich Pandaram Pillai and were definitely of the opinion that his father had lost a good opportunity. They called him an unwise person who did not know how to "live". Consequently, Diravi heard that one of his aunts offered to match Kuzhali with *her* son, even though she had three unmarried daughters at home. Who does not love money?

But within 10 days, Kuzhalarriangai's marriage was fixed with Thangappan, the son of Ekkiammai of the corner street. Thangappan was also Diravi's age. He too had passed his SSLC but was unemployed. He was quite a dandy and carried a small mirror and comb in his pocket wherever he went. He carried talcum powder in his handkerchief' people said; one could learn about men's fashion from him.' He was nicknamed "Symbalan"[1] in honour of his dandyism. He accepted it as his due and was said to be proud of it. He was not wealthy, was an only son and had no father to direct him or control his flashy ways.

Thangappan's father, Sonachalam Pillai, had been the driver of a Muslim merchant's lorry. He had died in an accident two years before. But Thangappan had refused to shave his head for funeral ceremonies, because he did not want to lose his beloved crop of hair. This was certainly a social revolution in the community and provided the necessary fillip to make him famous all over town. Diravi, thought that he was a fitting son-in-law for the newly rich. Diravi's family was not invited for Kuzhali's wedding at Kulachal. Only Mother shed tears at her inability to attend her only brother's daughter's marriage; no one else worried much about it.

After the wedding, it was rumoured that Thangappan found it difficult to recognise old friends. He had become important. After a few months, he moved permanently into his father-in-law's house. His mother was, however, alone in her old house, happy now that her son was married into a rich family. Thangappan visited his mother occasionally, dressed in the height of fashion: cowboy jeans, sunglasses, hair dressed in the finest way, in a car which proclaimed his new status as son-in-law. When Diravi saw him with Kuzhali, both of them pretended not to recognise him. They were vain people. The townsmen called "Symbalan Koi Thampuran". It was the custom of the Trivandrum palace to maintain a few men who would one day marry princesses of the royal family and their only distinction in life was that they were consorts of princesses. They were known as Koi Thampurans.

Once or twice in school, Moses reminded Diravi of what he had to do. He had made no headway, because many other things were happening, but now he had time to think about the plan in earnest.

Meanwhile, Kuttalam's textile shop was doing well. Kuttalam had some royal customers from Trivandrum to whom he sold the famous Eraniyal laced cotton at a huge profit. Diravi was pleased that his friend was doing well. His father was alive, though still helpless. Kuttalam devoted all his time to his trade, except when his father demanded his attention. Whenever he met Diravi, he renewed his request about Nagu.

At home, Nagu Akka was always busy with chores in the kitchen and backyard. She talked a bit to Salam, but rarely to anyone else. Diravi was old enough to guess for himself what Nagu's thoughts were like. Shortly after puberty, she had been married to Sevantha Perumal. She could not have known anything about marriage except that it was a change of dwelling. Within six months, she had been sent back home. She was a year or two older than Diravi, and like him, adult enough to think of her own plight. Salam's marriage prospects would suffer because of her sister's status as an unwanted wife. Even in the house, she could not talk frankly with anyone.

One day, when Diravi returned home, he found Aachi, his mother and the head-shaking old woman gossiping in the front verandah. He went behind the house to wash at the well and, coming back, saw someone lying on the floor in the backyard. It could not be Salam, for she did not leave the dark inner verandah. Mother and Aachi were talking in the courtyard. It could only be Nagu Akka. Diravi addressed Nagu. There was no reply; the figure did not stir. He was afraid…if he called Aachi or Mother, the head-shaking old woman would also come and make a hubbub. He went in, lit another kerosene lamp, returned to the backyard, and saw that it was Nagu Akka lying face down. She was perspiring, her exhausted face expressionless. The sight shook Diravi terribly. But by this time, the head-shaking old woman had left, Aachi and Mother came in, saw Nagu Akka, and were terrified. Aachi splashed water on her face and took her gently in her arms. In a couple of minutes, Nagu Akka recovered consciousness. She sat up and, on enquiry, confessed that of late she had frequently had similar fainting fits.

"I saw her the other day like this and thought she was tired," Mother said.

Aachi was sure that some ghost had taken possession of her. She recommended a puja in some temple. When Father returned from the fields and was told of it, he was greatly concerned and said, “Let us see the native doctor!” But Nagu Akka said there was nothing wrong with her and went about doing her work in the house.

Diravi thought that it was the right time to plan his campaign for Nagu Akka. He asked Father as to why he should not take his sister to the lady doctor, the wife of his colleague in school. “Moses is a very good and kind old man. His wife is a good doctor. If she examines Sister and gives her an injection, she would be cured immediately,” he suggested.

Neither Father, Aachi, nor Mother ever suspected anything; they consented immediately; it might be a good thing. Diravi was content that he was able to go ahead with the first part of his plan for his sister. Neither Nagu Akka, nor the family, nor the neighbours should get an inkling of his purpose in taking her to Doctor Rosammai’s quarters.

He told Moses the next Friday that he would take his sister to see the doctor on Sunday evening. Accordingly, Doctor Rosammai was ready for the them when they arrived. Rosammai was dark and past her youth. But she was a kindly soul and an efficient doctor. Without letting Nagu Akka suspect the real purpose of the visit, Diravi told the doctor of his sister’s fainting fits and asked her to prescribe a remedy. When they went into the examination room, he began to feel rather anxious. Moses sat with him talking of other things, but Diravi could not talk much. Yet what was there to fear?

Kuttalam had told him what he had learnt about Sevantha Perumal right from the source... What was there to fear?

A lizard was running about catching flies from behind the calendar. Moses had no children; the house was quiet. From the examination room, there was the sound of water running and hands being rinsed; the examination was evidently over. Moses was saying something which Diravi did not take in. The lizard had disappeared somewhere. The clock struck 5.

The door to the examination room opened. The doctor came out laughing, saying something to his sister.

"She has no trouble, really. She is very weak, that is all," the doctor told them casually and sat at her desk. "I shall prescribe some pills. Let her take them regularly."

Nagu Akka got into the cart first. Moses and the doctor followed talking to Diravi in English. Doctor Rosammai said casually, "Your brother-in-law is really an idiot." She said it almost in a whisper. Diravi looked at Moses who said, "Now you know for certain. Let us talk about it later, tomorrow."

How peaceful it was at the doctor's.

He was happy and at peace now, knowing for certain. The words, "Your brother-in-law is an idiot," massaged his mind.

When they arrived home, he told Mother and Aachi and Father that there was nothing wrong with Sister, but that she was weak and, that the doctor had prescribed some pills for her.

Twenty-six

The next day, Moses confirmed the information. There was nothing wrong with Nagu Akka. The fault, if any, was with Sevantha Perumal. Moses said, "You should not stand by anymore. He was either lying with an ulterior motive, or there is something really wrong with him. You should act now. I need not tell you anything more. You're an educated man."

The first part of the plan was over. The result was in his favour. Good. The second part of the plan would be to meet Sevantha Penlmal, tell him that a doctor had examined Nagu Akka and found nothing wrong with her. He should therefore take her back. Was there a way of doing it? Bow was he to arrange a meeting? Where? What was he to say? Perumal had wronged Diravi's family immensely; should he seek a meeting with him? Was it not undignified? If Perumal should bawl him out and insult him, what would he do? But Nagu Akka was not progressive enough to say that she would not consent to live with him. Even so, he could not afford to think only of his feelings and his own self-respect, when it was a matter which affected his family and his sister, Nagu. He was sure that he could defend himself competently now.

Diravi's resolution that he should meet Sevantha Perumal and talk to him was taking shape. But where, how, and when the meeting could be he was unable to say.

He trusted his elder brother-in-law, Tapasi Pillai, but even when Nagu Akka was in Sevantha Perumal's house in happier times, Diravi had not felt close enough to that brother-in-law. He was afraid of him. Perumal had been to their house on a few occasions and had exchanged only a few words with him. He would ask in what class Diravi was studying. Was he studying Tamil or Malayalam? That was all. After Nagu Akka came home, he had seen Sevantha Perumal a few times. But however much he disliked meeting him, Diravi felt he had to, because he had to solve Nagu's problem once and for all. He had to contain his own feelings, forge ahead objectively, and end her prolonged neglect. He tried to go to the shop once or twice, but it was too public a place. He set off to Perumal's house in Puthan Street, went courageously along, then walked past it, and went straight on to Kuttalam's house, saw *his* father and returned, his task undone. He did not want to let on, to his father that he was trying to meet Nagu's husband; there was no need for it yet.

Some weeks passed in indecision. Nagu Akka was taking the pills the doctor had prescribed and her fainting fits were becoming rarer. Diravi heard that Vadivu's mother had delivered a boy. This was usual; and he heard that Vadivu was in her mother's house for the delivery. He thought it was the best time to see Sevantha Perumal Pillai in his house.

Early in the morning, before many people were up, he walked straight to Puthan Street. A single door stood open. He knew that Sevantha Perumal slept on the first floor and he went up the stairs, straight to the bedroom. Sevantha Perumal was sitting in an easy-chair, his legs stretched out, lost in an account book. The early morning was pleasantly cold.

Diravi stood before him and coughed to announce his arrival.

Only then did Perurnal look up and see him. Perumal wore spectacles with thick lenses and his eyes looked big behind them. He was evidently shocked, his face a question mark.

Diravi deliberately stood silent for a minute. Sevantha Perumal closed the account book, placed it on the chair nearby, removed his spectacles, and looked up. Diravi had lost the nervousness he had felt at the start. He was not asked to sit. But that didn't matter—Brother-in-law was older by 15 years.

"Brother-in-law does not recognise me?"

Diravi was perspiring. He had not meant to call him Brother-in-law. He wiped the sweat off his face with his kerchief and smoothed his youthful moustache with his fingers.

"I recognise you. But what do you want of me?"

His voice was still authoritative, as if he were talking to the young school boy Diravi had been. Even if others did not know what Diravi wanted, Perumal could not say the same with any honesty.

"My sister Nagu—how long should she wait in our house for you?"

"I did not ask her to wait for me!"

"You may not have asked her to wait. But she is waiting for you. She has waited six or seven years now. She has had to live without her husband."

"Men older than you have talked about it and have understood what I did. It is a closed case." Perumal laughed dismissively, as if Diravi had said something funny.

"It is not closed. I am at an age now to know these things."

"You can talk it over with your father." His voice was angry.

"I have the right to talk on behalf of my sister to you," insisted Diravi.

"I see no need for it."

Diravi did not like his manner, but continued, "If your sister had been set aside by her husband like this, would you have kept quiet?"

"What is you intention now?" Sevantha Perumal asked, standing up. Diravi was taller by at least three inches, so Perumal had to look up to talk to him.

"It is her fate, written on her forehead. I can't do anything about it. It cannot be changed," he continued obstinately.

Diravi tried not to lose his temper. "I shall ask you only one thing, Brother-in-law. Don't get angry with me, but answer without hiding anything. She became aware of the truth about you, only after she married you. If she had set you aside and had married another, would you have agreed?"

This question came emphatically with the certainty of knowledge. Perumal could not reply. His helplessness was turning into anger, Diravi sensed. Before it could burst, he wanted to safeguard himself, He said calmly, "A week ago, I took Nagu Akka to the hospital doctor at Neyyoor. Lady Doctor Rosammai Moses examined her thoroughly.

"What?"

"*After* assuring myself that there is nothing wrong with Nagu Akka, I have come to ask you to take her back. You can draw your own conclusions from it," said Diravi firmly.

Diravi was sure that Perumal was aware of his position now. And Diravi continued, "If you want to, you yourself can talk to Doctor Rosammai."

"I don't need to talk to anyone," he said obstinately. Then after a minute's silence, he said, "You have come here with this tale, so that you can make the town believe that I said false things about your sister?"

Diravi also was giving way to his feelings. "I have no need to tell anyone any tales. As you yourself had said at that time, why don't you take her to a doctor of your choice and have her examined?".

"I shall not do anything like that. You need not talk to me about her!" he cried.

Diravi was thinking that as the doctor had said, Perumal was an idiot. "You drove my sister from your house under false charges. The trustees of the town were unable to do anything about it…I have been waiting to talk to you frankly and openly for a long time now…I have nothing to talk to you except about my sister …"

"Whatever you say I am not accepting her or taking her back."

"You said something false that day."

"Even then I shall not take her back."

"Why?"

"If I were to take her back, what would happen to my dignity, to my status in town."

"But my sister should not be sacrificed to preserve your dignity, your status!"

"You need not teach me about what should be done, what is just, and what my duty is ...I have some work. You can go."

"You have wronged. her. But we'll forget that if you will take her back and allow her to live along with Vadivu as your wife." Sevantha Perumal tried to interrupt but without allowing him to speak, Diravi continued sternly, "Take a week to think about it and let me know. I shall be ready to bring her here as soon as I hear from you." So saying, he turned and walked out.

There followed a week of anxious waiting for Diravi. He thought of Moses with gratitude for having opened his eyes to reality. He was glad he had been very cautious and patient when talking to his brother-in-law. If it helped to solve Nagu Akka's problem, it would serve. He told Moses what he had done. But Moses was not sure that he could make Perumal yield without going to court. Diravi had not told anyone home about his visit to Sevantha Perumal's house.

A week went by without any information from his brother-in-law. He waited a second week with great patience. Still there was no word. It was evident that Perumal did not want to right the wrong he had done.

Diravi passed his shop and thought of going in to talk to him. There were no customers yet, but the accountant was in the shop. It was not private or congenial enough for the intended talk.

But that night, he met Sevantha Perumal coming along after he had closed shop. He stood facing Sevantha Perumal, who also came to a stop. They stood under a street light. He did not speak, but walked ahead. Diravi too walked along with him.

"Diravi, I have nothing further to say."

"Then there is nothing between you and my Nagu Akka?"

"Nothing, there are no ties between us…"

"She wears a *thali*. what is the meaning of that?"

"Does she still wear it? Ask her to take it off and throw it away."

"Right. I'll ask her to snap it and throw it in your face: Then I'll find a man, a man I say, to marry her. After which she will bear a child. And then, what you said about her will be disproved to the whole town. How will you feel then?" asked Diravi unable to control his feelings.

For once Sevantha Perumal was nonplussed. He was afraid it would happen.

"How would you like your wife whom you set aside saying she wasn't a whole woman walking about in this town, with a child in her arms and another in her womb, happy with another fellow? What and where will your dignity be, your status, your honour among the men of your community?"

Diravi could not control himself. He knew he was incoherent, but he said what he thought he had to say. He was damp from head to toe.

Both were silent for a minute. Then Sevantha Perumal said, "Are you threatening me?"

"I don't need to threaten you. But if you don't take her back, I shall certainly get her married to another man. Things will happen as I have told you. Wait and see."

Diravi was sure that he would do it; he would overcome any obstacles; his family, his sister Nagu herself might object, but they would do what he asked of them, because Diravi knew he was right.

Perumal's eyes were red. Diravi's words went over him like a flame.

"Judging from what you are saying, you seem to have a person ready to marry her."

"Yes."

"From Puthan Street itself?"

Diravi hesitated wondering whether he should state it or not. But then why not?

"Kuttalam is ready and willing to marry her."

"Oho! That eunach..."

"That word is reserved for you."

Sevantha Perumal looked as if he would spring at him. But he controlled himself; Diravi was ready for anything.

Seeing his readiness, Sevantha Perumal walked along, as if unconcerned. Diravi walked by him and asked, “What is your final word?”

“It is already said. It is no concern of mine with whom she elopes.”

Diravi gripped Perumal by the collar of his shirt. But with an effort, he controlled himself and let go saying, “Pardon me!” He walked away, with a sense of great frustration.

Twenty-seven

He had betrayed his weakness at a moment of great stress, though for many days, he had planned to keep his temper under control no matter what the provocation. He had lost his balance for a moment, but had recovered almost immediately. Nothing untoward had happened. He asked himself whether Nagu would be happy with Perumal even if he had accepted her? But whether she would be happy or not everyone in the family, including Nagu Akka, wished to save their dignity and go back to the status of having their daughter as an accepted wife. They did not even think in terms of another marriage.

How long could Nagu Akka continue like this? It took Diravi almost a fortnight to attain his former state of mind; the talk-with Sevantha Perumal Pillai was over. Nagu had recovered from her fainting fits completely and had stopped taking the pills. No one in the house understood or knew the cause of Diravi's sudden meditative silence. He was thinking of how best to broach the subject, make Father and Aachi and Mother, and above all, Nagu Akka herself, accept the new decision. That was what was worrying him now.

In the meantime, Unnamalai Akka's son was put to school at Pazhavadai. When Father returned from Pazhavadai, he told them that his son-in-law's father and relative had proposed a bridegroom for Salam…the boy was elder son-in-law's second cousin's son—Bhagavati Appan. He had studied up to the eleventh class and was employed as a clerk in the Manavalakkurichi Sand Company. A good boy of equable temperament, he was comfortably off. It would be mean spending seven thousand rupees. The wedding could be celebrated in Pazhavadai. Both brother-in-law and uncle, his father, approved of the boy. Father had told them that he would consult with the others, but he was only partially interested in the talk of marriage. 'We celebrated a wedding. The daughter is with us still. Why contemplate another wedding?"

Diravi could not keep quiet. He said, "Even if we do want to do something about Nagu Akka, it is better that we celebrate Salam's wedding before we move in the matter." His Father could not have realised the implication of what he said…if he was to find a new groom for Nagu it was better not to be dependent on the community for anything. Diravi would be happier if Salam was married before any event in Nagu's life. His marriage would be the only thing left; he was not worried about the community's opinion. "But where shall I go for seven and eight thousand rupees now?" his father asked.

The interest on the loan that they had raised for his job in the private school was paid with great difficulty, month after month. Money was becoming a problem. "But if Salam is married, we have no other burdens. We can manage with what we get," Diravi suggested.

''Where are we to go for seven thousand rupees now?" asked Father irritably.

"Are you going to set about earning the money now? Manage somehow. This will be a good fellow for Salam because our Pazhavadai son-in-law's family to which he belongs is good. It will be a good match and will not lead to any trouble. Let us try to manage it as soon as possible," Aachi said, spreading clothes to dry in the courtyard.

"We have to clear the debt we incurred for my job," Diravi said, "Let us will this house to Salam and sell it to the groom. We can sell our lands to him too. Let them keep for themselves the dowry of seven thousand and give us what is left of the value. We can clear our debt. We can vacate this house some months after the wedding and rent a house in Karingal. We can get on somehow. If we lived in Karirtgal, I could make some more money giving private tutions."

This plan of Diravi's created a furore in the house, Aachi and Mother and Father—all were reluctant to sell the ancestral home. "But we are not selling it out of the family. We are selling it to our own girl and son-in-law. We can come here any time we want to visit." Diravi was bitter about the town and wanted to leave it.

The plan which was at first strongly rejected by all gradually became acceptable. Nothing else could be done to raise the money for Salam's marriage. Even Nagu Akka approved of the idea. Salam was sorry that they had to sell their house for her wedding. But born in a community where grooms could only be bought, there was no meaning in her tears and sentiments. Unnamalai Akka and her husband and his father were also pressing them saying that it was a good and rare match. The horoscopes were compared and found to agree.

When the do-wry was proposed in the terms that Diravi had laid out, the bridegroom's people were quite agreeable. The lands were to be handed over immediately, but the house might be vacated in a year or two, at the family's convenience, though the transfer was to be made to Visalam and registered.

All preparations for the wedding went ahead rapidly. What money they got from the sale of house and lands was enough to pay the dowry and clear the debt. There was still some money left to buy jewels and clothes and to pay for the wedding. The wedding was duly celebrated in Pazhavadai with all the traditional ceremonies and the usual pomp and happiness, the family crowds assembling. Salam went to her husband's house in Pazhavadai. Bhagavati Appan was a good person, who charmed everybody with his kindly speech and affectionate manner.

A storm was over. It looked like the calm before a new storm. Diravi was waiting for an opportunity to talk to Father at length, win his consent for what he proposed and then tell Aachi, Mother and Nagu Akka. Diravi chose an evening when Father was busy with his plantain grove. He had finished planting and was watering the place. He was deep in thought. The evening breeze was mild and pleasant. How Father had changed! Diravi could remember the days when Father was happy and always laughing; those days seemed faraway now. He was now growing bald; what hair was left was greying. He had lost most of his bodily strength. He lived feebly on his will power. He had changed since Nagu Akka's misfortune. He saw Diravi and said, "What is it, child?"

He loved this boy of his. His words proclaimed that love. Diravi wanted to tell him all that he had done. "I have not said something to you: I shall tell you what I have been planning. You should not quarrel or be angry with me," he said. With this preface he told his father about his fellow teacher, Moses; his wife, Doctor Rosammai and her examining Nagu and her conclusions. Then he told him about how he had met Sevantha Perumal and the talk he had had with him on two occasions. He did not conceal anything. Then he spoke about Kuttalam and his readiness to marry Nagu.

Diravi said all this in such a way that it did not irritate Father too much. He saw his Father listening silently, but he saw the face darken and stopped. It was Father's turn to speak; Diravi stood contemplating a tree. The sky above was darkening, it was silent and beautiful all round. The evening bell rang from the Pillayar temple. Father bowed in the direction of the temple, said, "SingaVinayaka! Vigneswara!... My lord!" and brought his palms together in obeisance. Diravi went away, walking slowly back home.

He did not approach his father for some days and he was outwardly calm. Father was evidently still thinking about what he had said. Diravi was restless. He felt he was not handling his classes right. Moses asked him what the matter was but he did not tell him anything. Four or five days passed. Diravi was tossing sleeplessly in bed. "Diravi," a voice called. Diravi sat up and said, "Yes, Father."

Father spoke in a whisper. 'You are worried about your sister. I am aware of your anxiety. That is why you took all these steps on your own for her..." Father sighed. "But if we do what you say, the honour of our family will suffer. It will dog us for generations to come. Have you thought of that?"

"If we leave it like this, would we not be doing Sister a great injustice? What her husband said of her is false. Should we allow this falsehood to spoil her whole life? Especially when we know it is false. Is it not dishonour to suffer it without rebuttal? Which is the worse dishonour?"

Father did not reply. The moon on high slid behind a cloud. Then the cloud passed and Father's face was visible to Diravi as he said, "I thought this would harm our family and our community. That is why I insisted that Salam be married off immediately, so that she should not suffer for it. Then we can face whatever happens!" he said with youth's complete courage.

Father had closed his eyes and was deep in thought.

When Diravi returned from school the next day, the house was in a hullaballoo. Father had evidently told his mother and wife what Diravi had planned. He never kept secrets from them. Mother, when she served him food, said, "You have done all these things by yourself bravely..." It was approval.

The sound of clothes being washed at the well stopped suddenly. It was Nagu Akka trying to listen to the conversation; then she too had been told. Good. It saved him some trouble, labour, and embarrassment.

Mother continued, 'You are the head of the family here after. Your word should be kept. Father also agrees, but will this happen?"

"It depends on us. We can make it happen," he said firmly.

"That Kuttalam—I hear he is not good; poor and almost an orphan," Mother said, her voice lowered.

Diravi raised his voice, so that Nagu Akka could also hear:

"He is no longer poor, mother. He has a shop that is doing well. He will take care of Nagu Akka as long as he lives. If I was not sure of it, I wouldn't advocate it." When he went to the well to wash his hands, Nagu Akka poured water over his hands. He looked at her, repeating to himself as if it were a mantra, "Believe me my sister, believe me, I shall find a way out for you. I shall. Believe me!"

No words were spoken between them, but everything was said. His burdens fell away. He felt that he had no need to speak to Nagu Akka about it; she too understood and was silently thankful. His mind was buoyant; his vow was about to be fulfilled.

It was more difficult to convince Aachi. She was down with her usual filarial fever. She could not believe that such things could happen and happen for the good. It was an axe at the root of tradition and convention in which Aachi superstitiously, but strongly, believed.

Aachi quarrelled with Diravi in her fever.

"Men, are like that. It is nothing new or to be wondered at. But when women too venture into these things, then the world is certainly coming to an end. It is the progress of Kali."

Twenty-eight

Before the town was aware of what was happening, Diravi wanted to celebrate his sister's second wedding. It was best kept secret till the actual happening or else the townspeople might interfere and prevent it from happening. Diravi promptly made all the arrangements. Kuttalam was ready; there was no postponing or delay from his side. It was decided that the wedding should take place on Velli Malai.

There was no need to compare horoscopes or the usual preliminaries but the month of Adi[1] was considered bad for a wedding. They waited for the month of Aavani[2]. Aachi was, however, unconvinced that this was for the good and was muttering in her general weakness and discontent as if the end of the world was near.

The steady deterioration in the status of the family, Nagu's fate, and the grinding poverty they lived in was enough to kill her spirit. Another important thing was the lonely helplessness of her brother Koonangani, whose life was like an empty theatre at the end of a play. His ears and eyes were failing him; he was becoming absent-minded; his mind wandered. He listened to what Diravi had to say to him about Nagu's second marriage but did not understand enough to make any suitable reply. Aachi wept continuously about what her brother had been and what he was now reduced to. She tried to help him but he bitterly rejected all offers of help in a spirit of total sacrifice. Aachi's body and spirit, not surprisingly, succumbed to all these stresses.

She was feverish nearly all the time; it was partly filarial which was usual and partly because of a broken spirit. Her sole sustenance was hot water which she drank only when Diravi brought it to her.

One night he heard Aachi cry out before dawn and saw that her bed was empty. She had gone out without waking anyone, fallen, broken her leg, and was whimpering in pain. They carried her back to bed and Diravi ran for the local *vaidyan*. Other vaidyas also came and saw her, but no one could ease her pain or promise recovery. It wearied her to stay in bed; she was accustomed to the daily household grind.

One day Diravi brought Doctor Rosammai to see her who thought that Aachi's blood pressure was rather high. She prescribed something but did not hold out any hopes. "She is old," was her only comment.

Month followed month. It was Aavani now; then it was Purattasi[3]. Aachi lay dying. Diravi was sorry that he had to postpone all his plans for Nagu Akka. He could not proceed with the wedding preparations while Aachi was on her deathbed. Kuttalam understood and was willing to wait.

Aachi had bed sores on her back and howled continuously in pain. They took turns attending on her, cleaning and medicating her. Now, even the betel-chewing had to stop. Her brother came to see her; he was shaken, but said nothing—they were two representatives of a bygone generation. Ammukutti Ammachi,' Sasi's father Krishnan Kutty, mother Thangammai, and Amminikkutti—all of them came. Sasi had passed his SSLC and was employed in the Nair Service Society Bank at Trivandrum. Amminikkutti was grown up and as charming as ever. Diravi's heart went out to her. He wanted to talk to her of many, things but could not. He talked to everyone, except her. When she came to take leave of him and said, 'We don't see Diraviamat all these days," he did not know what he replied; he was so confused. Her blue eyes asked him many things—but to none of them had he an answer ready.

Others came to see her and said, "Poor old woman. Give her all her favourite foods so that she might taste them before she goes on her last journey." But Aachi was not interested in tasting what she had always liked; she was indifferent. She laughed at times; she wept suddenly with no reason. She said things, recalling the past which she probably saw in her mind's eye.

Purattasi was followed by the month of Aipasi[4]. It rained continuously. And the wind howled without let up. Diravi sat watching her, lost in confused thoughts about what she had been, done, thought, and lived through. His generation too had to go the same way some time; that was the fate of all what there was to know of his family he had learnt from her. How full of pride she was! Full of stories and superstitions and faith too! He himself remembered many incidents in his own life when Aachi had figured as the heroine. And what a heroine! There was a strong bond between them. She had saved him as a child from a household fire when he lay in the cradle. Once when Diravi's schoolfellows were rioting, Aachi had come running all the way to school to save her grandson and shield him against all comers.

Two more months were to pass before she breathed her last. It was the month of Margazhi[5] and quite cold as it usually was at that time of the year. She asked for someone to read the *Ramayana* to her. She was breathing hard and with great effort. It was Nagu Akka who read the *Ramayana*. But the breathing stopped half way through the reading of the second chapter. They poured milk into her mouth, but it flowed down the side of her face. She could not swallow. She was dead. A ripe leaf from the book of life had fallen to the ground.

Like in a wedding, in funerals too the conventions and superstitions of a community take over; everything had to be done as it had been done before and ever will be. Aachi's body was kept on the same platform on which weddings were conducted. Sheaves of unthreshed grain stood upright in the courtyard. Incense sticks were lit. The town turned up to condole with the family. Women came laughing till they arrived at the house and then suddenly began wailing in sorrow. The young ones were really weeping. The barber was sent to all those relatives who had to be informed; telegrams were sent to those out of town. It was the barber who bought all the things necessary for Aachi's last journey. There was constant weeping in the house; if there was no weeping, the silence was abnormal.

Relatives began to arrive. Though bitter with them, Padmanabhapuram grandfather and his wife came; the house was crowded with mourners. The body was bathed, dressed and the vehicle for her last journey made ready with the usual skill. It was two in the morning when they carried the corpse out of the house; the conch was sounded. The funeral pyre was ready at the burning ghat; everything was in order. Father shaved his head and was ready to light the pyre. It was four in the morning, when they returned home.

In the house, there was a hubbub. No sooner had the bier left than some other relatives arrived and made a scene that the body had been carried away before their arrival. Andi Pillai and his group who came later still were prepared for a fight. He was quarrelling because he had been denied the right to see the body of his dear aunt before it was consigned to the flames. His womenfolk supported him loudly and with unspeakable words. Diravi was impatient with them. He said, "Take care of the living Koonangani Paatta. We are sure the dead can take care of themselves. Leave us if you don't like it..." They left abusing the family.

In a house of death; the only food served is boiled grain. Everyone partook of it. The townsfolk thought that Diravi had been rather high-handed with his uncle, but no one criticised him openly.

Twenty-nine

Even sorrow seeks a rhythm in expression. The songs of sorrow are as rhythmical as the songs of joy and marriage. In the 16 days following, Diravi became aware of the many types of songs with which women expressed their sorrow, chanting it at the same time, in chorus. How beautiful some of the expressions were, how evocative. One woman sang:

If she waited for a golden chariot,
the day would dawn
Oh my mother.
You set out on a chariot of flowers.
You set out all by yourself
Waiting for none of us, your dear ones
Oh my mother.
You did not wait for a silver chariot
The mother of virtue is gone
On her journey alone ...

The mourning song went on and on in waves of expression. It seemed that all the memories of Aachi would be exhausted in these 16 days, so that no one need remember her afterwards. The funeral and post-funeral ceremonies proceeded duly, Father doing everything with great devotion for the immense love he had borne his mother. On the 16th day, wailing was loud, long, and high pitched; it seemed it would never cease. It was almost like a wedding feast, except for the weeping. Father was made to shave, bathe, and wear new clothes. Kuttalam too was present at the 16th day ceremony. And those assembled noted the regard in which he was held by the whole family.

Diravi's school teaching continued as usual; when Aachi died, he had taken leave for just two days. He asked for another two days later, for Nagu's wedding.

Teacher Moses came to condole with them and gave Diravi the information that he was likely to be transferred to Shencottah. It was a shock, but on reflection Diravi thought it was for the better. He was glad when he overheard Moses discussing Nagu Akka's fate with Father. Father had accepted the idea already, but after talking to Moses, he was surer than ever that it was the right thing to do.

It was rumoured that Sevantha Perumal's shop had not been opened for two or three days. No one, not even Vadivu, knew where he was. But when he returned, he behaved as if he was slightly out of gear, as if his mind was unhinged. He spoke to no one but went to the shop and returned mechanically, lost within himself. It was said that Papathi even tried to have him treated for insanity.

But Diravi noted that Sevantha looked angry and bitter when he saw him by chance. Kuttalam reported that he looked at him as if he would have liked to kill him. Reporting it, he laughed happily.

Secrets could not be kept long in that town. Everyone minded everyone else's business. Like the rats and bandicoots that scurried from house to house in the dark, secrets too were common property. Everyone now seemed to know that Nagu's second wedding with Kuttalam had been arranged and they talked among themselves about it. The fishwife and the head-shaking old woman added fuel to the fire. If they had known of it before Aachi's death, they might not have spared the family even at the moment of death, thought Diravi. No one dared to talk of it to Diravi, but it was said that the community trustee, Vinayaka Perumal, told Kuttalam, "If they plan to celebrate a discarded girl's second wedding, did you not have enough self-respect to say 'no' to the offer. If you marry her, you will be set aside by the community." But Kuttalam was not to be daunted. He said, 'You and your community and trusteeship! You are all fools and knaves. What did you do for the family when that eunuch brought shame on a young girl. You come and talk righteously to me, you fool. Shut your foul mouth."

The town too heard it and talked even more about the coming event. Vadivu's mother was the only person who said something about it all in Diravi's hearing. "This Kuttalam is a useless fellow. Who can control him?" But Diravi did not want to pick a quarrel with an ignorant woman. He kept quiet. But he was sorry that he had to do this against the wishes of the town; if they were with him, instead of against him, how good it would be! The only thing left was to stand firm in his decision and to see it through, whatever the opposition.

Thirty

It was the first Tuesday in the month of Thai[1] and the dead of night.

Diravi lay tossing sleeplessly. Living without Aachi was dreary; he had grown up with her words ringing in his ears. Now, that voice was stilled. He imagined that Aachi was still with him, lying beside him, still talking, advising him, enlightening him on all things under heaven. There was no moon. The sky above was dark. There was a cold wind. Tomorrow was Wednesday; the next, Thursday. And on Friday, Nagu Akka's wedding would be over, her life would be forgotten. He had so far braved all the opposition he had encountered. He had ignored the ironic comments and stinging barbs aimed at him. He wondered at Nagu Akka's thoughts now. Thinking of the wedding ahead, he envisaged it as if it were happening before his eyes.

He was transferred to Shencottah. He had to join duty in ten days. Before that, everything here had to be completed. He did not want to celebrate the wedding in secret, as Sevantha Perumal had done. There was nothing to be ashamed of. A man had grievously wronged a woman—all womankind, in fact. Another man was willing to set it right; to give the wronged woman her due. There was nothing to be ashamed of about it.

The wedding invitations had been printed after consultation with the elders and duly distributed. If he had done things secretly, he would have felt that he was blameworthy. He had been straight and above board about it all. He had even gone out of his way to warn Sevantha Perumal about what he was planning.

After Nagu was married, they could all leave for Shencottah—his Father, Mother, and he. What else had they to do in Eraniyal. The time for handing over the ancestral house to Visalarn was also due. Let things be done in order. Moses also agreed that he had to take his parents with him to Shencottah. "Search for a good house for the three of you in Shencottah."

I can help you. I know a good many persons there," he said.

Diravi was afraid that their moving, this act of leaving with his parents, might be mistaken for cowardice. But that could not be helped. There was no one whom they could turn to now in Eraniyal. There were no families belonging to their community in Shencottah. It would be a good, new beginning. He need be afraid of no one in Shencottah—that was a relief. Brother-in-law and Sister had been told by letter of the decision; they were coming for the wedding the next day.

Diravi could not sleep. It was silent all round. But the silence was not complete. Diravi heard the distant strains of the *nadaswaram* from the east. Beyond Puthan Street was the Sollamatan[2] temple; it was a festival in the temple. They had a big festival with discourses, *villuppattu*[3], dances, and the like all through the night. The street residents contributed to the expenses and so everyone would be present at the festival. Kuttalam had called Diravi, but he had said, "It is better that I do not walk along Puthan Street now and appear at the festival."

He was suddenly in the midst of a nightmare without being aware of when he had gone to sleep. Someone was pressing his head into a sea of sand—throttling him with demonic strength. Was it his head of hair or beard and facial hair that interfered so. His eyes had gone bloody. Someone was laughing loudly and madly…something was rattling, the noise increasing progressively…the noise was increasing...

It was someone knocking impatiently at his door. It was not yet dawn. The eastern sky was not even grey; it was still dark. He opened the door.

Whoever was standing there said, "In Sollamatan temple..."

"What about Sollamatan temple?" He recognised the boy who was working in Kuttalam's shop.

"What happened?" he asked, alarmed.

"Master, master," sobbed the boy, Bhoothan. Diravi ran towards the temple thoroughly alarmed now and on the way, between running and walking, he got what Bhoothan had to say. In the festival after all the dances and singing was over, Ponnappan was possessed of Sollamatan.

The piper and drummer surrounded him and increased his frenzy.

In the midst of all this hubbub, Sevantha Perumal who had been listlessly wandering about as if he were senseless (as he had been all these days) shouted something horrible. But before anyone could recover, he snatched the whip and the leaves from Ponnappan's hands (symbols of possession), and ran away from the place and jumped into a disused well. The well was a ruined one without much water, but murderously deep though no one knew how deep, it was. It was said that many bodies had been thrown into the well and never recovered. No one dared to jump into the well after Sevantha Perumal Pillai. Vadivu came beating her breast and weeping loudly. She called for someone to help her crazed husband, out of the well. No one was prepared to. Vadivu was also preparing to jump in after her husband, but her father and others forcibly prevented her. Ekkimatan Pillai said, "I will jump in, but I won't be able to carry him. My arms are weak."

Vadivu ran to Kuttalam's house as if she knew what she was doing. Bhoothan said that he had followed her, running. Kuttalam was sleeping and Vadivu woke him up, told him her sad plight and cast herself at his feet. "You will have to help me save my husband..."

Whatever his bitterness about Sevantha Perumal, Kuttalam had a soft comer for Vadivu and he decided to help her. Kuttalam moved quickly, got into the well, and disappeared. No one had any clue about either Sevantha

Perumal or about Kuttalam for a long while. No one dared to venture after them into the well. No one knew what had happened. They stood helpless round the well. Vadivu was inconsolable. Two hours had elapsed since this had happened. The police were sent for. And Bhoothan, knowing that Diravi was a close friend of his master, had come for him.

When Diravi reached Sollamatan temple, it was dawn. The police van stood near the well. With the help of ropes and ladders in daylight, with the police leading the way a few others had also gone into the well. There were moments of expectation and anxiety, each person busy with his own thoughts. They came up. They hauled up a corpse—Kuttalam's. Diravi felt that the earth had split under his feet. He was hanging in the air. He remembered his nightmare—it was repeating itself when he was awake. He tried to rush to Kuttalam, but the police prevented him. They said they would have to do a postmortem before they could allow anyone near the body.

Sevantha Perumal too was brought up, but alive. He was bloody, gesturing wildly and madly. He was laughing loudly, maniacally.

Then, the news about it all leaked out little by little. Everyone guessed that Sevantha Perumal and his wife Vadivu had conspired to kill Kuttalam this way.

Sevantha Perumal might have been waiting in the well for Kuttalam. When he jumped in, Perumal might have throttled him and drowned him in the mud in the unused well. Sevantha Perumal was already known to be deranged.

Now, they might declare him insane and irresponsible for his actions. He might escape the death penalty.

Nothing, however, 'was definitely known. Nothing was proved. But much 'was hinted at. And the town saw Sevantha Perumal being taken to Trivandrum under police escort, his hands manacled in the van of the mental ward of Ooalamparai Mental Hospital. He was laughing demoniacally, they said.

***

It 'was like a bad dream. Nagu Akka, Father and Mother, and, of course, Diravi himself left the house and the street and got into the bus. They were more dead than alive. For the last time, they looked at the street where they had lived so long and minded their business. They would never see it again. The temple bell of Singa Vinayaka rang and the 'waves of sound floated through the air and reached them, lost in thoughts of their own as they sat in the bus. Diravi noticed that Father as usual turned towards the direction of the temple, lifted his palms and joined them in obeisance.

Glossary

One

1. **Singa Vinayaka temple:** The deity in this temple at Eraniyal is Simharakshaka Vinayaka, meaning the Vinayaka who saved Narasimha (the half-man, half-lion incarnation of Vishnu). Vinayaka is the elephant-headed deity of the Hindu pantheon.
2. **Aachi:** The equivalent of the respectful appellant for grandmother (Paatti).
3. **karpaga:** In Hindu mythology, the karpaga tree grows in heaven. It gives the celestials whatever they want.
4. **white clothes:** Orthodox widows wear only white, sometimes using a single length of cloth believing everything else to be an affectation or decoration.
5. **Vignesware:** Another name for the Lord Ganesha, meaning "remover of obstacles."
6. **cowdung-water mix:** This mix is like a mild insecticide; also, since all the products of a cow are sacred to Hindus, this too is something good and auspicious.

Two

1. **nadaswaram:** A double reed wind instrument. Loud and strenuous to play it is usually used outdoors in temples, processions, festivals and at auspicious functions.

2. **kolam flour:** It is an Indian practice to draw geometric decorative patterns on the ground just outside the house, with rice flour.

Three

1. **Paatta:** Grandfather.
2. **Akka:** Elder sister in Tamil.

Four

1. **inji:** Ginger; a common term describing a short temper.
2. **Krishna woman:** "Krishna" refers to a caste in the Kanyakumari district.
3. **horoscope:** The horoscope of couples who have not even met are appraised for compatibility before further discussions on their wedding.

Five

1. **break five coconuts:** As thanksgiving, coconuts are flung on the ground before the deity.

Six

1. **kottai:** Equivalent to 160kg
2. **thali:** The symbol of marriage worn by the bride on a yellow cord around her neck
3. **kumkum:** Powder of a brilliant colour. The authentic item is prepared by grinding cinnabar. A sign of caste and/or marriage depending on how it is used.
4. **kolava:** A shrill ululation by women at the start of some auspicious event.
5. **nichyatham-boolam:** Engagement performed ritually.
6. **erection of the first pillar:** The start of rituals.

Seven

1. **kabaddi:** A popular Indian game played with two teams. One team tries to seize a member of the other team who repeats the word "kabadi" without drawingbreath while he sets out to touch every member of the opposing team.
2. **Pillayar:** Another name for Lord Ganesha. A crude form is fashioned from cowdung, and worshipped as part of a ritual.
3. **muhurtham:** The auspicious time when a wedding is solemnised.
4. **kandangi:** A long chequered sari about five-and-a-half metres in length.
5. **kanakambaram:** Orange coloured flower.
6. **mulmul:** Fine muslin.
7. **murukkus:** A savoury made of gram and lentil paste twisted into different shapes before it is deep fried.
8. **alenge:** A sweet meat made of jaggery and rice flour.

Eight

1. **mundu:** Dhoti.
2. **Etten:** Colloquial Malayalam for elder brother.

Nine

1. **Pillai:** A title conferred for skill in accountancy. Also for valour.
2. **Anna:** Elder brother.

Ten

1. **Velli Malai:** Literally, silver hill.
2. **amrit:** Divine nectar.

3. **darshan:** The act of gazing at the deity and the special adornments of a temple.

Fourteen

1. **Atha:** Old woman; granny, grandmother.

Fifteen

1. **rasam:** A thin spicy soup with a tamarind paste.
2. **vakil:** Tamil for advocate.
3. **mantras:** Incantation; a particular combination of words which when recited is supposed to have an energising effect, empowering the person who chants them.
4. **masalas:** A mix of spices.
5. **Onam:** The harvest festival in Kerala.

Sixteen

1. **seemantham:** A religious ceremony usually performed during the eighth month of a woman's first pregnancy at her husband's house.
2. **puranas:** The sacred writings on Hindu mythology and folklore.
3. ***Tiruppugazh, Tiruvembavai, Ramayanam, Mahabharatham:*** Sacred literature.
4. **chakram:** Coin.
5. **rajyam:** Kingdom.

Seventeen

1. **Kali:** According to Hindu cosmology the last and most evil age; the other three being Krita, Treta and Dwapara.

Eighteen

1. **Poorattathi:** A celestial body, a star, said to be ruled by Aja Ekapad, the one-footed serpent.
2. **Uttarattathi:** Another of the 28 stars in the Indian system.
3. **"touched the pots":** The various stages of a woman's biological cycle are considered "unclean" and she is said to be in a "polluted" condition. In practical terms, she gets the rest she needs during these times.
4. **Dewaswom:** The trustees who control the ancient temples in the erstwhile Travancore State, Kerala.
5. **payasam:** The traditional sweet/pudding served at the end of a feast.
6. **Bhagavati:** The pre-Vedic manifestation of the Mother-goddess, widely worshipped in Kerala.
7. **singhi**: Two small metal drums.
8. **pepper chilli mix:** According to the theory of pranic forces, to wave this mix over and around a person effectively draws out any negative vibrations from her/him.
9. **Benares:** The holiest place of pilgrimage for Hindus.

Nineteen

1. **SSLC:** Secondary School Leaving Certificate.
2. **Hiranya:** Could apply to either Hiranyakasipu or his twin Hiranyaksha. The destruction of the demonking Hiranyakasipu was the purpose of Lord Vishnu's fourth incarnation, Narasimha (manlion). The killing at twilight was so violent that the blood of the Lord's victim is believed to have soaked the sky. The reddish tints we see at dusk are a daily reminder of Hiranya's defeat. Also applicable is the equally gory defeat of

Hiranyaksha by the third incarnation of Lord Vishnu, Varaha (boar). The spirit of the dying demon as it flashed through space is supposed to have lit up the whole universe with its brilliance.

3. **Vaidyan:** A native (ayurvedic) physician who treats patients with Indian drugs i.e. medicinal herbs and leaves.

Twenty

1. **kozhukattai:** A preparation of steamed rice flour dough, either filled with jaggery and coconut or tempered with savoury condiments and seasoned with salt.
2. **pandal:** A temporary shelter/hall partially enclosed, usually with a decorative roof of thick cloth and dried coconut fronds.
3. **padaiyal:** Food offering to gods, here *kozhukkattai*s.
4. **ponkal:** Preparation of cooked rice and lentils garnished with fried cashnut, coconut and seasoning.

Twenty-one

1. **prasadam:** Traditionally floral and edible offerings are made to a deity. Later it is distributed amongst devotees as the deity's acknowledgement of devotion received.
2. **Sastan:** Lord Ayyappan.
3. **blasts:** In some temples, the offering is in the form of fireworks.
4. **Rohini:** A star in the Indian zodiac.
5. **turmeric:** A dilute paste is applied to the face, neck and limbs of maidens and women who are not widows, to lend an auspicious glow.

Twenty-two

1. **Nagaraja:** Lord Siva.
2. **bhangra:** A vigorous dance performed with abandon and enormous gaiety in rural Punjab.

Twenty-three

1. **Kurukshetram:** The region where the *Mahabharatha* war is believed to have been fought. The word refers to a place of conflict.

Twenty-four

1. **Vijayadasami:** Vijaya=victory, dasami=tenth day. The last day of the ten-day festival. The puja to Goddess Saraswai is performed on the ninth day.

Twenty-five

1. **symbalan:** A typical mixing of language codes, this word is derived from "simple".

Twenty-eight

1. **Adi:** Tamil equivalent of the Malayalam month Karkadakam which is the last month of the Malabar or Malayalam Era known as Kollam Varsha beginning from mid-July and ends in mid-August).
2. **Aavani:** Chingam, first month of Kollam Varsha, which is considered to be auspicious (from mid-August to mid-September).
3. **Purattasi:** Kanni, second month of Kollam Varsha, from mid-September to mid-October).
4. **Aipasi:** Thulam, the third month of the Kollam Varsha, from mid-October to mid-November.

5. **Margazhi:** Dhanu, the fifth month of the Kollam Varsha (December to January).

Thirty

1. **Thai:** Makaram, sixth month of Kollam Era (from 14 January to 13 February).
2. **Sollamatan:** Short form of Sudalai Maadan i.e., the deity of the cremation ground (Lord Shiva).
3. **villuppattu:** A programme of folk music. The main singer sings the folk songs while simultaneously plucking the string of a long ornamental bow with small bells.